The Quincy Bay Quandary

Dan DeKoning

DEDICATION

This book is dedicated to the Geocaching community.
To hiders, finders, and those behind the scenes.

See you on the trail!

The Quincy Bay Quandary

CHAPTER ONE

Drake Decker was so busy watching the plane's shadow pass over the houses, office buildings, and highways below them, he didn't catch the question.

His seatmate, Allie Ashe, tapped him on the shoulder to get his attention. At first, he didn't react, so Allie had to tap progressively harder to get him to notice her.

"Earth to Drake. Hello? Anyone home?"

Drake's head turned toward her, and his hazel eyes met her green ones.

"Are you nervous?"

"About what?" Drake asked.

"Seeing her again. It's been a long time."

Drake made a face like he'd bitten into a lemon stuffed with tart cherries.

"It's only been eight months. That's hardly any time at all."

"Yeah, but perhaps she's forgotten about you by now," Allie teased. Aside from working out, going to Broadway musicals, and geocaching, messing with Drake was one of her favorite activities.

"It's not like we never talk. We text every day, and video chat at least four times a week," Drake said.

He looked at Allie, who, despite trying to keep her straight face, cracked a wide grin, and finally he recognized she was trying intentionally to rile him up.

"Thanks, Allie," Drake said as he rolled his eyes. "As if this flight isn't long enough, you're going to torture me even more by messing with my head?"

Allie giggled, then slapped Drake on the thigh. "Sorry, just trying to entertain myself."

"And you couldn't do that by reading that in-flight magazine? The one with the cover hanging half off and the crossword puzzle already done, usually completed by two different people?" Drake said.

Allie rummaged through the seat pocket for the magazine and when she pulled it out, she noted the cover was indeed missing the top corner. She skipped right to the last page and paged backward through all the airport terminal maps until she came to the crossword. Sure enough, it was already done. Someone with a red pen filled out more than a dozen answers, all the simple ones, she noted, and a different passenger had completed the rest in black ink.

"How did you guess?" she asked.

"Because they're always like that. And chances are, if you're flying into a city that's featured in an article, someone has torn that article out as well."

"That makes no sense to me. Why not just take the entire magazine at that point?"

Drake shrugged. "No clue. I've never done it. I also don't understand why we didn't drive instead of fly."

Allie released her ponytail from the dark blue scrunchy she wore. She gathered her long red locks together, including the strands that had wrestled free over the course of the last few hours. She pulled her hair tight and bundled everything back into a ponytail.

Drake watched her, and in return, he took off his Tennessee Titans baseball cap. He ran his fingers through his military precision cut blond hair and returned his hat to his head.

"You know why. There's a convention I'm going to in two weeks and it would take us forever to drive to Boston and back," Allie said.

Drake shook his head. "We've been through this. Nashville to Boston is only seventeen hours one-way. Had we taken turns driving, we would have gotten there in one long day."

Allie nodded and gave him a sarcastic smile. "Would you have wanted to find some geocaches along the route?"

Drake shrugged. "Probably. Only to get out of the car and stretch our legs. Or there might be one at a gas station or restaurant we would normally stop at, anyway."

"Mmm hmm, sure. Remember that time we traveled to Knoxville, only a two-hour trip from home? How long did that take us?"

"I don't remember," Drake said, then turned back to the window.

"I remember. Six hours. We almost missed the event because you wanted to stretch your legs so much."

Drake returned to looking at her and smiled. "Hey, that wasn't all me. You're the one who wanted to visit those EarthCaches along the way."

"That was different," Allie said.

"How?" Drake pressed.

Allie's nose crinkled as she attempted to find an answer in her head. "Well, because they were pretty. Don't you remember how gorgeous those waterfalls were?"

"Thanks for proving my point. It's not all me, and you know it. So, you ask, how long would it take to travel seventeen hours across what, seven states? I'd guess three days."

"That's not too bad," Allie said. "I would have guessed five days. Six at the most."

Drake laughed and patted her leg. "Yeah, that's probably more like it. It's all right though, we've got the money, so it was good to treat ourselves to a flight."

The previous fall, Drake and Allie took part in an exclusive geocaching competition. They were one of only ten teams vying for a fifty-thousand-dollar grand prize. Although a couple of teams tried to cheat their way to the prize money, Drake and Allie had come out on top. More important than the cash, though, Drake had met his new girlfriend.

"You still would have preferred to drive, right?" Allie asked.

Drake nodded, then shrugged.

"What's the plan if we ever get there?" Drake asked. "I mean, other than geocaching."

"Well, I love history, especially American history. Since Boston is crucial to the birth of America, I'd like to spend a couple of days taking in the touristy sites. I've never been to Boston before. What about you?"

"I'd like to check out the Salem witch trial locations. And isn't Lizzie Borden from up there somewhere? I'd like to see her house," Drake said.

"You want to delve into the macabre? Is Geneva into all that creepy stuff?"

"Not really, but she said she'd be up for whatever. We're the tourists in her city, after all. I'd like to do other stuff, too. Maybe go see the Red Sox if they're in town. Or take a boat tour. I've never been on a boat tour. Oh, and of course, we absolutely must eat some authentic Boston clam chowder."

Allie stuck out her tongue. "Yuck, you can keep the chowder. Clams are nasty. I'd rather have a nice Boston creme pie."

"I've heard people say you can tell if the clams are fresh if there's sand in the chowder."

Allie made a soft retching noise, then smiled at the person across the aisle from her who was eying her warily. "As if the chowder wasn't bad enough, you want sand in it? No thanks, I'll stick to a burger. Medium rare. No sand."

"Oh, I forgot, Tuesday night we're going to the symphony. Geneva's playing that night and she wants us to go," Drake said.

"What? You should have told me that before we left Nashville. I didn't pack my symphony dress!" Allie protested.

"Symphony dress? Does it come with long white gloves, high-heeled black designer shoes, a clutch purse, and a pearl necklace?"

"Of course," Allie said. She tried to hold the moment, then laughed. "Okay, I don't own a symphony dress."

"Do you own any dress?"

Allie slapped Drake's arm. The report was louder than she expected, and when she looked over at the man across the aisle, she caught him glancing at her over his business magazine.

"Of course. I own a dress," she whispered to Drake. "Well, okay, maybe not a dress, per se. It's more of a long skirt. But I have a really nice blouse and jacket to go with it."

"Really? I've never seen you in that outfit."

"That's probably because I only wear it to funerals and weddings, and we don't go to those together, do we?"

"Well, we might someday." Drake threw Allie a wink that she easily caught.

"Drake Decker, you're not thinking of proposing, are you? After eight months? Are you serious?"

Drake nodded.

"No? Really?"

Drake nodded again, but he couldn't hold his straight face and chuckled. "Got you."

"You're such a jerk. Just for that, I might have to drop some hints that you are indeed thinking about the idea of a wedding."

"You wouldn't?" Drake said, as a look of deep concern

passed over his face.

Allie nodded. She took an interest in straightening the materials in the seat pocket in front of her.

"No. really?"

Allie smiled. "Got you back."

"You're such a jerk," Drake said.

"And that's what you love about me."

Drake turned back to look out the window to see if they were any closer to their destination. He hated to fly, partially because he didn't like being cooped up in a tin can, and partially because he had to give all his control over to someone he'd never met. Of course, he'd heard all the statistics about flying being the safest form of travel. However, between the events of 9-11, the Miracle on the Hudson, and a lifetime of movies he'd seen involving air crashes, he was always leery about getting on a plane. His canned response was if the engine failed in his car, he could always pull over to the side of the highway and call for roadside help. The pilot couldn't really do that at thirty thousand feet in the air.

Drake closed his eyes and leaned his head against the cool, oval plane window. Allie was right. It would take them several days to make the drive a third of the way across the country. He was also excited, yet anxious, about seeing Geneva. It was true they talked in one form or another every day and shared text messages and video chats over the last few months. Drake's biggest concern was if the passionate flame they kindled in the Arizona desert had died off. He also worried if they were still as good a match being together in the real world as they were in the virtual one.

Drake glanced over at Allie and secretly wished she'd declined his invitation to go with him. He wasn't worried she'd interfere with his private time with his girlfriend. Rather, Drake worried she would get the third-wheel feeling that people often got in situations in this. He had to invite her along for the ride.

She'd talked about visiting Boston for forever, and he believed if she found out he went there without her, she'd never speak to him again. And that was after she buried him in a hard to get to holler in the Appalachians of eastern Tennessee.

Drake had a surprise for her, though. Geneva's friend and geocaching partner, Ingrid, planned on joining them for lunch. He saw that Allie and Ingrid had sparked a pretty wonderful friendship when they first met back in October. According to Allie, they'd only kept in touch a few times a month via text, but Drake was certain Allie would be happy to see Ingrid. Also, if he could convince Allie and Ingrid to venture off together to find caches or explore the city, that would be all the better. It would be more time alone for him and Geneva.

Drake focused on the landscape and watched the city leave his view, replaced by the blue of the Atlantic Ocean. Even from as high as they were, he could see the whitecaps atop the waves, and the uncountable number of boats either heading away from or toward the shore. His adventurous side wanted to get on one of those boats and feel the power of the ocean beneath his feet. Realistically, though, he was prone to seasickness, so he sensed he'd spend most of the voyage with his head over the side of the boat.

The overhead bell dinged, and the captain's voice came over the intercom with the message that they'd be landing in fifteen minutes. Around him, the passengers and crew impatiently got their respective acts together.

"Did you know that most airplane accidents happen during takeoffs and landings?" Allie asked.

"Does that go along with most accidents happening within five miles of your house?" Drake countered.

"I don't know. It was just a statistic I read once," Allie said.

"What do you want to do when we land?" Drake asked, desiring to drop the plane crash topic.

"Get off the plane," Allie deadpanned.

Drake gave her a grin. "No. I mean after that."

"Go to the second women's room I find."

"Second? Why not the first?" Drake asked.

"The first one will have a line out the door. At the second one, I'd have a decent shot at actually getting a toilet. You wouldn't understand the struggle since you're a man."

Drake took some mock offense at the comment. "Hey, what's that supposed to mean?"

"It means you're a guy and you can pee anywhere. I've seen you mark so many trees, I think you're part beagle. You probably go into a men's room and share urinals, but women don't have that luxury."

Drake thought about it. He had been to more than one stadium where the men's room featured one wall to wall stainless steel trough for men to do their business into. He thought twice and smartly dropped the conversation topic all together.

"No. I mean when we're out of the airport. Want to get some food, or find some caches, or see some sights?"

"What time is it?" Allie asked.

Drake checked his watch. "Almost nine. We've got the entire day ahead of us."

"I don't need food. I can hold out until lunch. What if we can find a cache or two near something historical and kill three birds with one stone?" Allie asked.

Drake nodded. Since geocachers often hid geocaches near sites of historical interest, they could usually do both at once. It was an excellent strategy they often applied whenever venturing away from home. Otherwise, they'd never think of visiting Abraham Lincoln's boyhood home in Kentucky or the world's largest ball of twine in Kansas. Based on how scenic the spot was, either the geocache or the location took top billing. They'd found a magnetic keyholder in a guardrail in Wyoming once. Although the geocache wasn't all that unique or spectacular, the view of Devil's Tower from ground zero was.

"Sure. We can see if Geneva has any suggestions," Drake said. "She'd know a spot right off the top of her head."

There was a slight jolt as the wheels hit the runway, followed by the whine of the air brakes being deployed. They coasted straight until they slowed, then the pilot navigated the plane to the terminal. Drake watched as the gate numbers continued to rise and knew, based on his luck, the plane would stop at the gate farthest away from everything.

The plane slowed as it approached the jet bridge and around him the distinctive metallic sound of seat belts unfastening filled the air. The plane had barely come to a stop when people around Drake and Allie rose from their seats.

"Aren't you going to stand up?" Drake asked.

Allie leaned over so she could see down the aisle. "Not yet. Relax. The door hasn't opened yet, and since we're way back here, it'll be a good ten minutes before we can move, anyway."

"How can you be so sure?"

"Experience. Because of FAA regulations, there has to be an older person in the first five rows who needs help to retrieve their bag from the overhead bin. And then we have to wait for them to get into the aisle and put on their hat and coat before anyone can pass them."

"That's a regulation, huh?"

Allie nodded. "We're just lucky this is our final destination and we're not connecting with a half hour or less to catch the next flight. In that case, the law says there has to be an elderly person and a single mother with a baby and multiple bags somewhere in the first five rows."

Drake shook his head at her.

"Hey, don't blame me. Look it up."

The duo sat still. When Allie noticed the line move, she rose and retrieved Drake's carry on and set it behind her and then pulled down her suitcase and set it in front of her. Then she fished her backpack out from under the seat and threw it over her shoulders. As she waited for her turn, she extracted the handles on both pieces of luggage. Once the aisle was clear, she pushed hers ahead and dragged Drake's bag behind her until he was out of his seat and ready to haul his own suitcase.

Once they were out of the jetway and in the gate area, Allie removed her backpack. She did a couple of yoga poses to stretch her limbs as Drake fished his phone from his pocket and texted Geneva.

Ready to go, they pulled their luggage behind them as they navigated their way through the terminal and the hordes of people walking in their direction. Drake noticed Allie didn't even hesitate when she passed the first women's room they found, which had a line stretching out into the open space of the corridor. They hiked on for five more minutes. When they came to the next women's room, Drake moved off to the side and watched over Allie's bags while she took care of business.

"Did you hear from her?" Allie asked upon her return.

"Yeah. She's waiting for us at the cell phone lot. I'm supposed to text her again when we get outside. Apparently, security likes to keep the pickup zones moving along quickly."

They followed the signs to baggage, went down an escalator, and a few seconds later they were outside in the warm June weather. Sure enough, airport security personnel were at several places waving their hands and blowing their whistles. They tried to keep the flood of passenger cars, taxis, and airport shuttle buses moving at a good clip. All the while keeping a close eye on the pedestrians trying to cross the road to the parking garage.

"She'll be here in like thirty seconds," Drake said.

"You know what she drives?"

"Navy blue Nissan Rogue."

Drake had barely finished answering when a blue blur swung up to the curb next to them. Geneva popped out of the SUV, opened the trunk, then greeted Drake with a hug and a kiss, and then gave Allie a hug as well.

A security guard whistled at Geneva to get her attention, then pointed at her car and motioned for her to pull away. In response, Geneva gave him an air kiss, then got back in the driver's seat while Drake and Allie tossed their bags in the trunk. Thirty seconds later, everyone had their seatbelts on, and Geneva drove toward the airport exit.

"Where to?" Geneva asked.

"Allie likes American history. Do you know of a geocache we could visit with a historical angle to it?"

Geneva looked in the rear-view mirror and glanced at Allie. "Of course. We'll go where it all started. Perfect way to begin your trip."

CHAPTER TWO

"Did you have a pleasant flight?" Geneva asked as she raced along the interstate, weaving in and out of traffic like a NASCAR driver. Drake held on to the grab handle above the door with a grip tight enough to whiten his knuckles.

"We got here without incident, so I consider it a great success," Drake said.

"Allie, how's your knee? Ingrid told me you're one hundred percent now."

Allie leaned forward from the backseat so she could hear better. The windows were open, so the whoosh from the passing air combined with the highway noise made it difficult to hear anything in the front seat.

"It's more like eighty percent. I had to have surgery to fix a tendon in there, and it'll take another few months until I'm fully recovered. Until I heal, no more long hikes, climbing mountains, or running marathons for me."

"You won't have to do any of those things this week, and I can guarantee you won't have to worry about a scree pile the height of a five-story building."

"Good," Allie said and settled back into her seat. It had been eight months since the accident, but she still dreamed of tumbling down that giant hill out in the desert. Unfortunately, her fall was only a couple of days into the competition. Her stubbornness and competitive nature kept her going at it for the rest of the week, and although they'd won the top prize, Allie often wondered if it was worth it. She realized she only had herself to blame. Drake, as her geocaching team partner, had asked her multiple times if she wanted to keep going, and she agreed to press on. She couldn't quit. In a previous career, she spent ten years as a U.S. Navy medical corpsman, and for eight of those years, she served with a Marine unit. If it was one thing she learned in those eight years, it was Marines didn't quit.

In the front seat, Geneva offered her hand to Drake, and he took it without a hint of hesitation.

"I'm happy you guys came out here. It's good to see you in person," Geneva said.

"Me too. I'm sorry I didn't have time to come out earlier." Drake squeezed her hand, but not too hard. There was an incongruity in her touch. Her hands were silky and supple, yet each fingertip on her left hand wore the rough telltale calluses of a musician.

"Where are we headed?" Drake asked.

"Out to Lexington, where the revolution began. There's a multi-cache out there that should take us an hour, maybe a little more, then we'll head downtown. Ingrid is meeting us in the city for dinner tonight."

Geneva laid on her horn to let the driver in the Mercedes beside her know she existed and bullied her way over to the exit ramp and left the highway. After another five minutes of assertive driving, Geneva turned into a parking lot and grabbed the first spot she saw. She turned off the car and sat back in her seat.

"Welcome to the Lexington Battle Green, where the initial shots kicked off the Revolutionary War. There's a multi-cache here that will take us to a few of the historic sites in the area. Here, I copied down the geocache code for you."

The trio got out of the car, and Drake and Allie went for their cell phones and opened their favorite geocaching apps. It wasn't long before they each found the geocache page for the multi-cache.

"Oh, my, this is a five-part cache," Allie said as she read the description. "We need to get some numbers from the monument and then use those to calculate the coordinates for the next stage."

Drake shook his head. "That's on you. You know how I feel about math."

Geneva laughed at him. "Come on, my big hero. You can handle some addition for me, can't you?"

"I'm not so sure about that, Geneva. There's multiplication in here too, although since it's by zero, I think Drake may have a chance of figuring it out without the calculator," Allie said. She hit Drake on the shoulder and tugged him toward the large monument in the center of the green.

"Can you imagine being here when the first shots of the war rang out?" Allie said when they got to the monument.
Geneva nodded. "It must have been a scary time. One day you're carrying on with your normal life, and the next you're in the center of a huge armed conflict."

While the women chatted, Drake circled the monument, searching for the numbers needed for the geocache. Once he'd completed the circle, he had a list of values written in a pocket-sized notebook. He passed his notes to Allie, who responded with a mock huff, then dramatically rolled her eyes. Without asking, she leaned forward and snatched the pen Drake had protruding from his baseball cap right above his ear.

To be helpful, Drake read out the calculations from the geocache description while Allie did the math. Soon, she had all the numbers they needed to go to the next stage. She added a waypoint with the new coordinates into her app and looked at the updated location.

Allie showed her screen to Drake and Geneva. "Next stop is over two miles from here. That can't be right."

Geneva borrowed Allie's phone and opened the map function. She studied it for a second, then handed the phone back. "Nope, that's right."

"How do you know?" Drake asked.

Geneva smiled. "Because I've already done this multi-cache."

"So why don't you take us right to the final, and we can skip all the steps?" Drake asked. "It would save us a ton of time and energy."

Allie stepped in and grabbed him by the arm. "No way. That would take away half the fun. Where's your sense of adventure?"

They got back in the car, and with no need for directions, Geneva drove them five minutes up the road and pulled into a parking lot with room for only four vehicles. They left the car and sauntered over to a small area surrounded by a short rock wall in the shape of a horseshoe. At the top of the horseshoe was an old plaque, green with oxidation. The story written on it recounted the tale of when British troops captured Paul Revere while out on his famous midnight ride. To the left and right of the plaque were more recent informational signs that added additional details to the event.

Drake looked at the cache description and alternated between his phone and the signs. He jotted down the needed numbers as he found them, and while he did that, Allie immersed herself in the history at the site.

Since there was no math to do for this puzzle, Drake entered the coordinates into his phone and projected the next waypoint.

"You ready to go?" he asked.

"Don't rush me, Duck-man, I'm learning something here. For example, did you know Paul Revere wasn't alone on the ride? There were a couple other guys with him, and of the three, he was the only one caught by the British?"

"So how did he get all the glory, then?" Drake asked. The stone wall was only a couple of feet tall, so he sat down on it and waited for Allie to finish reading the three markers there. He knew from previous experience that she liked to slow it down sometimes and take in the things surrounding her.

Drake was the opposite of her in that he usually liked to rush from geocache to geocache to increase his find numbers as fast as possible. Allie often had to insist that he stop for a few minutes so she could pause and read a historical marker or wander around a cemetery. Allie liked to take pictures of the scenery, or step into a local history museum for a few minutes. Since she did it, regardless of whether he wanted to, Drake had no choice but to wait for her.

"Where are we going next?" Allie asked as she turned to him.

"About a mile away. Are you okay to hike that?" Drake said.

"No need," Geneva said. "I can get you closer. Where we're going next is part of the national park, so we can get into the parking lot nearby, but there's still enough of a walk involved to stretch your legs."

Less than three minutes later, the trio were strolling up a paved lane. Drake periodically checked this phone to make sure the distance was getting shorter, an indication they headed in the correct direction. Within ten minutes, a saltbox style two-story building came into view. The exterior wood stain matched the same color brown as many of the trees that surrounded it. The only hint of color was the small panes of glass in the large windows that were bordered with white trim.

"This is amazing," Allie marveled as they stepped up to the main door of the tavern. "I love old buildings like this. I wonder if it's original."

"It is, indeed, ma'am," a park ranger answered. He stood just inside the door waiting for them. Rather than the typical tan and green of the National Park Service uniform, the ranger wore an outfit of full colonial garb, from the tricorn hat on his head, right down to the wide buckles on his shoes.

"About sixty-five percent of the tavern's original structure is here. Although it had some changes over time, the NPS restored it back to the way it looked in 1775," the ranger explained. "Care to come in and look around?"

"Would I? I'd love to. Can you give me a quick tour?" Allie asked.

The ranger took off his hat and bowed. "It would delight me to no end. Please, step this way."

Before entering, Allie turned back and addressed Drake and Geneva. "Are you guys coming with me?"

Drake waved her off. "Nah. Knock yourself out. While you take the tour, Geneva and I will find the coordinates for the next leg."

Allie smiled, then stepped over the threshold and into the building.

"Shall we?" Drake asked.

"Sure. What do we need?"

Drake scanned the description. "Let's see. We need the number of panes of glass above the entry door. The number of cross beams on the tavern room ceiling. The number of barrels in the pantry. Um, the number of spokes of the spinning wheel in the kitchen. The number of windowpanes in the parlor divided by five, and the number of large windows on the front of the tavern. These are some odd things to count."

Geneva nodded. "Yeah, but this building is closed for half of the year. When I did this cache, I had to look inside the windows to get the answers. It would probably be easier if we just walked through, well, except for the last one. We can get that answer from here."

Drake took a few steps away from the building, quickly counted the number of windows, and jotted down the answer.

"I can do the first one from here, too. It's seven. Come on, let's go inside."

Drake and Geneva passed the ranger and Allie as they rushed through the third room they got to. They stopped long enough to get the information they needed, then stepped back out into the sunlight.

Drake completed a few quick calculations and entered the numbers into his app as a new waypoint. "Four miles?"

Geneva cocked her head while she thought, then nodded. "That seems about right."

Drake took her hand, pulled her close into an embrace, and leaned in and kissed her. "I can't tell you how much I've missed you."

"Even though we talk to each other almost every day?"

"No, silly, I mean, I've missed seeing you in person. Holding your hand, kissing those soft lips of yours."

Geneva gave him a kiss, then pushed him away. "You're such a goofball, you know that?"

"He knows it, but he can't help himself," Allie said as she exited the tavern. "Where are we headed next?"

"Another tavern. It's a few miles from here, so we'll drive it," Geneva answered.

A quarter of an hour later, the three stood outside of the Munroe Tavern, a two-story wooden building painted red with white-trimmed windows.

"All the numbers we need will be on the outside of the building," Geneva said to Allie. "Drake and I can look for those answers while you go on in. There's a little museum in there that contains, among other fascinating things, the very table George Washington sat at when he ate here."

"The actual table? No way," Allie said.

"Way," Geneva answered.

"Okay with you if I go in and take a peek, Drake? I won't be too long. I promise."

Drake looked at his watch. "Okay, I'll give you five minutes. If you're not out in five, we're leaving without you."

Without responding, Allie made her way to the entry and went into the building.

"That was mean. Five minutes?"

Drake smiled. "I've got to put a time limit on her, or she'll be in there all day. Don't worry, I'm sure that five will stretch into twenty or more. She'll rush, but she'll do her version of rush and come out when she's ready. Let's get the information we need while we wait on her."

Drake and Geneva circled the building and got the numbers they needed, which included the number of chimneys and how many doors. They also had to count the number of windows on the west side of the building, and the number of words on the fourth line of the sign hanging by the driveway's entrance.

After they got all the required data, Geneva and Drake returned to the car and waited for Allie to appear, and ten minutes later, she did. She slipped into the back seat, excited by what she'd seen, and regaled the couple with all the details of what they'd missed. Of course, she spent most of the time discussing the Washington table and several documents relating to his trip.

"Are you going to be like this all week?" Drake asked as Geneva started the car and maneuvered her way across the driveway to the main road, checked for traffic, then pulled out.

"Like what?" Allie asked.

"Fangirling, every time we come across some trivial item related to the Revolutionary War?"

Allie sat back in her seat and crossed her arms. "You simply don't appreciate history. You never do."

"No. I do. I just like it in moderation is all," Drake said.

Allie didn't have time for a retort, because Geneva turned again, then parked the car in a large public park.

"Here you go, last stop for this cache. I'll wait here while you two venture off into the trees," Geneva said. She rolled down all the windows, then shut off the engine.

Drake and Allie exited the car, and Drake checked his app and headed off toward the large grove of trees in the distance. The park was a nice one, with gentle, rolling hills, a walking trail, and several benches and picnic tables scattered throughout. There were a hundred yards of a grassy area with tall, individual oak trees that stretched to the sky, and the grass gave way to a dense pack of trees in the park's rear.

"How many more feet?" Allie asked when they reached the spot where the grass ended, and the grove began.

"Fifty," Drake answered. "Okay, into the fray, we go."

Drake stepped into the woods with Allie following three feet behind him. She learned from experience to keep far enough back so that if he moved a branch out of his way to get through, it wouldn't spring into its original position and hit her.

Drake walked for ten feet, stopped, checked the direction and range, then started again. After fifteen more feet, he stopped again, looked up to get his bearings, and started again. The app he used sent out a ping like a submarine's sonar, and as they got closer to ground zero, the pings resounded faster. When they arrived at the coordinates, the pings came rapidly, one after another, so Drake clicked off the app and slid his phone into his pocket.

"We should be right on it, so look around and see if there's anything that jumps out at you," Drake said.

"Sure, of course. There's like twenty trees in a thirty-feet radius, along with five stumps that I can see from here. This should be a simple one to find. Were there any hints on the cache page?"

Drake retrieved his phone and checked the hint. "It says wooden you like to know, and it's spelled like tree wood, not like the would you would use if you said you would do something."

"That's zero help, and confusing besides," Allie said.

"The cache is a small size, so that should tell us at least something," Drake said.

Drake and Allie split up and started examining the trees in the area for a geocache hanging from a limb, or perhaps a large hole in a tree in which to place a container. Allie also checked the tree stumps, which is a favorite hiding spot for many geocachers in the woods.

After ten frustrating minutes of not finding anything, Allie walked around a tree and stopped.

"It's over here."

Drake crossed over to her, and she pointed at the birdhouse attached to the tree when he got near her.

Fake birdhouses are also a favorite hiding spot. Typically, the first sign that it wasn't a real birdhouse was that the cache owner blocked off the entry hole with wood or a mesh. The hole was almost always painted black. From the glance of a casual hiker, it looked like a real birdhouse, and they'd be none the wiser that there was a secret treasure inside.

The birdhouse had a hinged roof, so Drake lifted it and extracted a small plastic box. He opened the box and took out the paper log from inside, signed it with his geocaching name, and passed it to Allie, who added her nickname below Drake's. She handed the paper back to Drake, who then put everything back the way they found it.

Mission accomplished, they took a more direct route out of the woods and started their walk back to the car.

CHAPTER THREE

"How was that for you?" Geneva asked when Drake and Allie took their seats and belted up.

"Good," they said, almost in unison.

"Oh, wait, I forgot to tell you something. The final is a birdhouse," Geneva said, then grinned.

Drake took off his hat, removed a small stick that was stuck in it, and tossed the stick out the window. "Thanks for the hint. Where are you going to take us next?"

"We can head downtown right away, but I was wondering if either of you wanted to go to Bunker Hill or tour the USS *Constitution* before we do. They're fairly close to each other."

Drake checked his watch. There was plenty of daylight left. "Would we have time for both?"

"Of course, depending on how long you'd want to spend at each location. They both have museums nearby, and you can climb to the top of the Bunker Hill monument and go on the *Constitution* and explore the vessel."

"Let's do both," Drake said.

Geneva went back into beast-mode as she navigated the

local roads and dipped back onto the interstate that circled the northern part of the city. Within forty minutes, she pulled into a spot next to a park and rolled up all the windows.

"We can walk to both from here. Where to first?"

"Which one is farther? Let's do that one first," Allie said.

"That would be the boat. Everybody out. Make sure you don't have any valuables showing through the windows."

They got out and stepped into the park.

"What's up with the red brick road?" Drake asked.

Cutting through the park in a straight line was a path of red bricks, set two wide, in the concrete.

"That's the Freedom Trail," Geneva explained. "Tourists primarily use the trail to get to most of the primary historical sites in Boston. The route we're on will take us to the ship. Had we gone that way," Geneva turned around and pointed at the bricks headed in the opposite direction, "we would end up at Bunker Hill."

"That's a good idea," Allie said. "I bet it really cuts down on people getting lost."

"True. It also cuts down on traffic. It's less than three miles long, so the trail is pretty easy to walk. Of course, some people still drive it."

Allie spotted a memorial in the distance and attempted to veer off toward it, but Geneva caught her by the shirtsleeve and brought her in close.

"It'll still be there when we get back. I'm in a two-hour parking spot, so we need to move it along," Geneva said.

Allie nodded, then stepped back onto the road. Geneva guided them down Adams Street and turned on Chestnut. They walked a couple of blocks, then followed a pedestrian underpass which took them under a highway. When they got to the other side, they spotted the mast of the three-hundred-year-old frigate in the distance. They followed the red bricks, and soon they were at the entrance to the ship.

They secured tickets for the next tour, but had fifteen minutes to wait, so Drake pulled up his geocaching app and checked for nearby caches in the area. "Hey, there's a virtual twenty feet from here."

"Sweet," Allie said, "what do we need to do to claim it?"

Virtual geocaches, unlike the other geocache types, had no physical container to locate. Instead, it had other qualifications to mark the geocache as a find. Sometimes a geocacher had to answer questions specific to the location. Other times, they needed to post a photograph of themselves, and often there were other requirements. Virtual caches were such that geocache owners could place them in areas where regular caches couldn't go, such as in federal lands.

"You need to upload a photo of yourself with Old Ironsides in the background. That's it," Drake said.

"Easy enough," Allie said.

Drake held up his phone, got into position, and was ready to snap a selfie when Geneva stopped him.

"Hey, why don't you two get close, and I'll take a photo of both of you," she said.

"You sure?" Drake asked. "Would you want to get one too, or…"

Geneva nodded. "Yep, I already logged this one."

Drake and Allie positioned themselves, so the USS *Constitution* was in the background, then stood shoulder to shoulder.

"Okay, smile," Geneva said.

The pair smiled, and while they waited for Geneva to take the picture, Allie formed a V with her fingers and put her hand behind Drake's head to give him rabbit ears. Geneva noticed it coming, and waited a second until the fingers were in place and snapped the picture.

"Okay, you're done," Geneva said as she handed Drake his phone back.

Drake glanced at the picture long enough to spot the ship in the background and sent the picture via text to Allie before he logged the geocache as a find for himself. Once Allie received the photo, she used it to claim the find on the virtual for herself.

"C'mon, time to board," Drake said.

The three queued up in line to get on the ship and waited to be called aboard. Once there, they were free to roam around the ship. True to her nature, Allie rushed ahead to see everything she could see.

Below deck, they saw the white canvas hammocks that acted as beds for the sailors. Beyond that, they found the captain's cramped quarters, and a small dining parlor, among other rooms and areas on board. Most impressive were the well-maintained cannons that gave them the impression the ship was ready for war at any second.

Back on the top deck, they walked among the cannons and took in the sights of the Boston skyline in the distance.

"What's that over there? The thing that looks like the Washington Monument?" Allie asked as she pointed to an obelisk.

Geneva walked over to her side to see what she was pointing at. "Ah. That's Bunker Hill, our next stop."

"I have to admit, I'm really impressed by this ship," Allie said, leaning closer to Geneva. "And don't tell Drake I said that."

"Why not?"

"He loves these things, and I can't tell you how many battleships, submarines, and aircraft carriers he's had me tour with them. I find some of them interesting, but after the third hour of hiking up and down the stairs across ten decks, it gets to be a little much. You get what I mean?"

Geneva laughed. "Yeah, I get you. I visited the *Yorktown* in Charleston with a friend once, and I was ready to leave there after thirty minutes. It got so hot down in those lower decks I felt like I was in an oven. It wasn't even a warm day out, and I still sweated right through my shirt."

"This one I don't mind. I like the wood, and it's so well maintained. Did you see that leather furniture down below?"

"Not bad for the oldest ship in the fleet," Geneva said.

"What are you ladies talking about?" Drake asked as he joined them.

Geneva winked at Allie. "Simple girl stuff. Ready to head over to the museum?"

They disembarked the ship and followed the wharf to the museum, where they walked through exhibits on the history of the USS *Constitution*. They also learned what it was like to be a sailor during the early years of the U.S. Navy. After forty-five minutes of reading practically everything and a brief visit to the gift shop, the trio left the museum. They stepped back on the red brick road and headed back in the direction from which they came.

"Hey, there's a cache here," Allie said as they approached the underpass.

"Really?" Drake stopped and opened his app, and Geneva did the same.

"You sure?" Geneva said. "I haven't found one around here."

"Yep, there it is. A brand new one," Drake said. "Looks like it's in the middle of the tunnel. Has a terrain rating of one-and-a-half, and a difficulty rating of four. Cache container is the other type."

The three slowed their gait as they walked into the underpass. Since there were no obvious places to hide a geocache, they concentrated on the walls. They checked for any cracks, holes, or depressions; anywhere something could hide. After ten minutes of looking, Geneva turned the light of her cell phone on and pointed it at the wall, lighting up a small pink object attached to the wall.

"Is that it?" she asked.

Allie got closer. "It looked like used chewing gum to me, but I'm not going to touch it. You touch it."

Geneva shook her head. "I'm not going to touch it, you touch it."

Allie shook her head. As one, both women glanced over at Drake, who was busy looking over another area of the wall five feet from them. "Drake!" they both said as one.

"What?"

"Come check this," Allie said.

Drake joined the women and saw the gum. "I don't want to touch that."

"You're too late. Allie and I both called it before you."

Drake rolled his eyes, then examined the surrounding ground. Not finding what he wanted, he left the underpass and returned a few seconds later with a stick in hand.

"Stand back. I'll take care of this."

Drake put the stick end next to the gum and pushed on it. It wiggled a bit but didn't pop away from the wall like he expected. He tried again from a different angle, got the same results, and handed the stick to Allie. He reached up, put his thumb and forefinger around the gum, and pulled. The gum pulled free, and Drake found he wasn't holding gum at all, but a rubbery pink plastic that only looked like chewed gum. Attached to the fake gum was a small plastic vial.

"That was sneaky," Geneva said.

"Thus, the difficulty of four," Drake answered. From inside the vial, he extracted the logbook, and jotted down his geocacher handle and passed the paper and pen to Geneva and Allie. Once everyone signed the log, he rolled it up, stuck it back in the vial, and closed the lid.

"Put your light up against the wall, Geneva."

When she did, Drake looked over the area again until he found the small hole from where he pulled the cache. He inserted the vial into the hole and pushed the fake gum against the wall, so it looked like a careless person had stuck it there.

They continued their walk and stopped when they reached the open air and took a moment to log their finds. When they got back to Winthrop Square, Geneva checked her watch and saw they were short on time. While Drake and Allie checked out the nearby soldier's monument, Geneva moved her SUV around the block and found another parking spot. Within ten minutes, she rejoined her friends.

It didn't take them long to walk the three blocks to the Bunker Hill area, and they stopped at the corner.

"The museum is right behind us," Geneva said. "That's the monument over there, obviously. There's a virtual geocache at the top, and all you need to do to claim it is take your picture with the 294th step."

"What if you lose count?" Allie asked. "Have to come down and start all over again?"

Geneva laughed. "That would be cruel, wouldn't it? No need to worry about that. They painted the number on the top stair. All you need to do is climb up all the stairs, take a picture, enjoy the view, and come back down."

"I assume you've already done this one, too?" Drake asked Geneva.

She nodded. "Last summer."

Allie scanned the monument from the bottom to the top. "That's like a twenty-story building."

Geneva nodded again. "Yeah, a little more, probably."

"You want to do it, Drake?" Allie asked.

"You know I do. I'm never one to stand down from a challenge. What about you?"

Allie looked over the monument again. "You know I like an easy virtual. However, in this case, I think I'm going to pass. There's no way I'm going to put my knee under the strain of six-hundred steps."

Drake nodded. "I don't blame you. Do you mind if I go?"

"Of course not. Knock yourself out. While you're doing that, I'm going to check out this museum. If you're not back by the time I'm finished, I'll go across the street and sit on those stairs and wait for you."

"Sounds like a plan. What about you, Geneva? Coming with me, or staying with Allie?"

Geneva didn't hesitate with her answer. "Sorry, Drake, you're on your own with this one. The second I got down from doing that climb, I vowed I'd never do that again. Make sure you take it easy, okay? Don't try to be a hero and run up and down it in five minutes. It's a lot harder than it looks."

"Okay." Drake leaned over and kissed Geneva on the cheek. "I'll be back when I'm back, and I'll see you guys later. Enjoy the museum."

Drake turned, crossed the street, and bounded up the stairs toward the monument.

"Shall we?" Geneva asked.

Allie and Geneva stepped into the museum. After thirty minutes of learning about the Battle of Bunker Hill, the monument's construction, and the obligatory visit to the small gift shop, they exited.

"That was pretty interesting," Allie said.

"It was. I've never been in there before," Geneva admitted. "Ice cream?"

Allie looked where Geneva was pointing and started walking toward the vendor. "How can I resist getting ice cream from a food truck featuring a smiling ice cream cone on the side?"

A few minutes later, Allie and Geneva were sitting on the steps where they said they'd meet Drake. Allie had a waffle cone filled with mint chocolate chip soft serve while Geneva preferred a cup stuffed with rocky road.

Allie concentrated on her cone and quickly rounded off the ice cream to prevent it from melting and dripping over the edge. Once she was certain she had prevented the crisis, she looked over at Geneva.

"You don't have to worry about me. Like I told you in Arizona, Drake and I are only friends, and nothing has changed about that over the last eight months. I'm not a threat to your relationship."

Geneva finished her bite of ice cream, then took a moment to play with the rest of the dessert in her dish. "I know. He's said the same thing to me. I don't think there's anything romantic going on between you two."

"Good," Allie said. "You should also know that while we're here this week, I'm perfectly capable of entertaining myself, so don't let me offend you if there are some nights when I want to have dinner with myself and a good book or catch a movie with me and me alone. You can't expect that I'm going to be with you guys twenty-four hours a day while we're here."

Allie winked, and Geneva snickered.

"Well, okay. You're being kind of tough on us, but if you insist on leaving the two of us by ourselves, then I guess we'll just have to accept that." Geneva scraped the rest of her ice cream into the spoon, then ate it. She set the spoon into the cup, wiped her hands with a napkin, then balled it up and added it to the cup as well.

"Is there anything special you want to do while you're here?" Geneva asked. "I tried to get some ideas from Drake, but he wasn't helpful."

Allie was close to finishing her cone, so she waited until she'd eaten the final bit of it before she answered. "Well, I could go for more ice cream."

Geneva smiled. "You'll ruin your dinner."

"Yes, mom," Allie said. "Seriously, I'm just along for the ride. Find some geocaches, see some historical stuff, that's good enough for me. Maybe take in a Red Sox game. Are they in town this week?"

"I'm not sure. I could check, though. Are you a big baseball fan?"

Allie shrugged. "Not huge, but I enjoy going to a game now and then. I've been to Cincinnati, St. Louis, and Atlanta for games, so I'm always looking for other parks to visit. It's fun to see what the locals do at ballparks. You know what I mean?"

"Not really. I've always assumed that everyone just sings "Take Me Out to the Ballgame" during the seventh-inning stretch."

"Well, there is that, but some places do more than only sing the song. For example, in Milwaukee, they have sausage races."

Geneva's brow crinkled. "What's that?"

"They dress people up as sausages, like a bratwurst and a hot dog, then race around the field."

"Sounds weird," Geneva said.

Allie shrugged. "It's what they do."

Allie wiped her mouth with a napkin, then stood and picked up Geneva's empty cup. She walked over to the trash can, threw out the refuse, and walked back.

"I wonder what's taking him so long," Allie said.

"He's probably half-way up, regretting his life choices," Geneva said.

Allie smiled. "I know I would be. I hate doing stairs. You know, I hated stairs even before I hurt my knee. Hey, here he comes."

Geneva stood and looked toward the monument and picked Drake out of the crowd. He was walking slowly; the pep lost from his step. It took him much longer to get to them than it normally would.

"Hey, honey, how was that?" Geneva asked when he finally got to them.

"I have to admit, it was a magnificent view."

"How are you feeling?" Allie asked.

"My legs feel like jelly. I never want to do that again."

"Hopefully you remembered to take the picture," Allie said.

Drake turned and looked at the monument, then slapped his forehead. "Actually, I did forget. There were so many people up there, I couldn't have if I had remembered. I probably would have been trampled had I sat on the steps for a photo. I'm going to get some ice cream from that truck over there."

"No, you can't," Geneva said.

Drake scowled. "Why not?"

Allie smiled at him. "Because you'll ruin your dinner."

CHAPTER FOUR

They ambled back to Geneva's SUV, with Drake protesting the entire time. With a sigh, he collapsed into the passenger seat while Geneva started the car.

"What would you guys like to do next? I know of a great multi-cache in a park south of Boston. It's about a five-mile round trip," Geneva said.

In response, Drake groaned like a giant had hauled off and kicked him in the family jewels.

Geneva turned and smiled at him. She glanced in the rearview and saw Allie holding a hand over her mouth, trying not to break out into laughter.

"So that's a no?" Geneva asked. "How about something easier?"

Before anyone could answer, Geneva's phone rang. She pushed a button, and it connected to the car's Bluetooth.

"Hello?"

"Geneva? This is Stacy. Jonathan just called. He's going into surgery early tomorrow morning to get gallstones removed. Gallstones. Can you believe it? I didn't think people still got those. Anyway, he won't be available on Friday, so can you step in for him?"

A wide grin crossed Geneva's face, but she tried to hide the excitement in her voice. "Oh. I'm so sorry about Jonathan. I can sit in for him."

Stacy's sigh of relief came over the car speakers. "Thank you. Hey, do you think you could come down to the theater? I'm here now, and it shouldn't take more than a couple of hours to go over everything."

"Right now?" Geneva confirmed.

"Yes. Would that be a problem?"

Geneva looked over at Drake, who shook his head no. "No. That's fine. I'll be there within an hour. Does that work?"

"Certainly. See you soon." Stacy clicked off without saying goodbye.

"Yes!" Geneva yelled as she tapped excitedly on the steering wheel. "Yes, yes, yes, yes, yes, yes!"

"Good news? What's going on?" Drake asked.

"Jonathan has gallstones! That's great!"

"Yes. We overheard, and I think Jonathan would disagree on how great gallstones are," Drake said.

"Yeah, yeah," Geneva said. "Anyway, Jonathan's our normal conductor, and the backup is out of the country, so I'm going to do it. Can you believe it? I'm going to conduct a symphony!"

"Great, honey, I'm proud of you. It's the big break you've been waiting for."

"I'm happy for you, too," Allie said from the backseat. "It sounds like an excellent opportunity."

"Anyway, you know I need to go in for a couple of hours. We need to review the program, and oh, my, I just realized I'll need someone to replace me. I was supposed to be the first chair cello. I guess I can move everyone up a chair and have Brad fill in the open seat, right?"

Geneva looked over at Drake, but he simply shook his head. "I have no clue what you're talking about. Would you be able to drop us at our hotel before you go?"

Geneva laughed. "Of course. I won't kick you out at the next corner and expect you to find your way. The hotel is a couple of miles from here, will take less than five minutes to get there."

Geneva had covered half the distance when the Boston traffic converged around her like a tight blanket. Geneva cursed herself when everything slowed to a glacial pace, and her hand went to her forehead in frustration. She tried to adapt by honking her horn a few times, but only got honks from other cars in return.

"Sometimes I really hate this town," she said as she slammed on the brakes as someone cut her off.

As they inched along, Geneva played tour guide and pointed out sights of interest. She also mentioned restaurants she'd eaten at, complete with reviews of what she thought of each of them. After twenty minutes, she finally turned off into the guest check-in area of the hotel.

"Boston Common is like three blocks from here. There are a few geocaches scattered around, mostly virtuals, but there are a couple of mystery caches, and other types as well. If you don't want to geocache, there are plenty of attractions to check out. And of course, tons of stores if you want to go shopping," Geneva said as Allie and Drake pulled their luggage from the trunk.

"I'd be fine with a shower and a nap," Drake said. "I'm a little tuckered after that climb."

"Great." Geneva leaned over and gave him a kiss. "I'll call you as soon as I'm finished and we can all go to dinner, okay?"

Without waiting for an answer, she waved goodbye, got back in the SUV, and inched back into traffic.

Drake and Geneva walked into the hotel, and although it was still a little before three, it delighted them to discover that their rooms were ready for them. They took the elevator to the fourteenth floor, and Allie unlocked the door to 1432, while Drake moved on to the room next door.

Drake pulled the folding luggage rack from the small closet, placed it next to the dresser, and set his bag on top of it. He zipped it open and pulled out the travel kit and hauled it to the bathroom sink. Drake was about to strip off his shirt when he heard a knock on the door. He moved to the door, opened it, and stuck his head out. He looked both ways down the hall, but he saw no one. As he closed the door, he heard another knock and realized it came from the inner door to his left. He unlocked the deadbolt and opened the door.

"We have adjoining rooms, isn't that cool?" Allie said.

"Yeah, sure."

"I've never had adjoining rooms before. I'll leave my door unlocked, but knock first if you want to come in, okay?"

"Sure thing," Drake said. "I'll do the same. I, uh, was going to take a shower and lay down for a bit."

"Yes, I know. You said that downstairs. I only wanted to let you know I'm going to go out for a while. I want to take a walk, see what there is to see. Give me a jingle when Geneva calls, and I'll meet you back here, okay?"

"Okay, be careful out there."

Allie closed the door, turned on the lamp next to the bed, checked to make sure she had her room key, then left the room.

She walked out of the hotel and stopped when she got to the sidewalk. There, she had to decide which way to go. Left or right. Since they had come in from the left, she turned right, walked to the end of the block, then looked down all the streets at her hiking options. Things seemed to open up a bit to the right, so she headed in that direction. Allie passed several restaurants and stores as she walked, but nothing captured her attention until she came to a bookstore.

It was a small bookstore, and the picture window was barely eight feet wide. She was walking at a good clip, and her brain finally registered what she'd seen in her peripheral vision once she'd already passed it. Allie came to a stop, then walked backward, and turned to look in the window.

The window display showed only one book she recognized as a recent release. The other books in the window were older editions of classic literature. She spotted a copy of *A Tale of Two Cities*, *Robinson Crusoe*, and a *Batman* comic book that looked to be from the late sixties.

Intrigued, Allie opened the door and stepped into the shop. Above her, a bell rang when the door opened, and rang again when she closed the door behind her.

"Can I help you?" the store owner asked.

She'd been so focused on looking at all the potential treasures on the shelves, she didn't notice the small man sitting behind a counter.

"Not really. Is it okay if I just look around? I love old bookstores."

"Certainly. If there's anything I can show you, let me know."

Allie took a brief look around at the layout of the store. The bookshelves were made of wood, well-stained and polished, and were six feet tall. They reminded Allie more of library shelves rather than those normally found in a retail bookstore. They stood close enough together such that only one person could comfortably be in an aisle at a time. Handwritten labels on the ends announced the type. The fiction labels had subclasses of genres; the non-fiction titles divided into subjects.

Usually, Allie liked to roam bookstores in a snaking pattern. She'd go down one aisle and up the next, but in this store, each aisle ended at the wall, so Allie had to go down and come up the same aisle.

The first aisle she stepped into enveloped her in a cocoon of old-book smells. The aroma, a mixture of a faint odor of vanilla combined with the scent of old leather book covers and glued spines. As she walked along, she noticed the owner cared for the books, at least in the first aisle. There was no dust present on either shelf or spine, and there was no musty odor present. She was in the mystery section, surrounded by Agatha Christie on her left and Arthur Conan Doyle on her right. She noticed several copies of *And Then There Were None,* the first Christie book she remembered reading, and the one that got her hooked on the author. Although there were at least a dozen copies on the shelf, none were the same. Roughly a third was hardcover, and she pulled from the shelf what she considered the prettiest one of those. It had a maroon binding, and the title stamped in gold on the spine. Allie opened the cover to the title page. Inside was a bookmark featuring the store's name, Stanford's Stories. On the bookmark was a sticker with the book's name, the publication year, which was 1940, and the price, which was one hundred and fifty dollars.

Allie gently closed the book, returned it to the shelf, and selected a paperback version with a creased spine instead. The bookmark inside told her that printing was from 1991, and was only five dollars, much more in line with her budget for a used book.

She put the book back on the shelf, continued to the end of the row, waiting for something to catch her eye. When she got to the wall, she turned around and strolled up the other side.

The next aisle's label told her she was in for romance and westerns. Since she was a reader of neither, she skipped it and stepped over to the next, which featured biographies. Allie often enjoyed a fun biography, so she ventured down the aisle hoping to find something interesting on one of the founding fathers she hadn't yet read. She saw volumes on George Washington, John Adams, Paul Revere, and Benjamin Franklin. Every book she pulled had a price tag of twenty dollars or more, even for later printings and editions that weren't in the best shape. For comparison, she turned around and picked a book at random. It was a leather-bound edition from 1931 on the life of Richard I, and that volume carried a cost of a more modest fifteen dollars.

In the history section in the next aisle over, she discovered the same thing. The cost of a book about the thirteen original colonies' history was fifty percent higher than a book about the history of Texas or England.

The last aisle was what Allie really enjoyed: the world of discount, mass-market paperbacks. She picked up the first book she found, opened the cover, and without regard for any other information, looked at the price. Two dollars! She returned the book to the shelf, then scanned the spines for authors she enjoyed. Allie spotted several, and since they all wrote mysteries or thrillers, they were all clumped fairly close to each other. She bypassed the ones she'd already read, and pulled out a few that she either hadn't read, or couldn't remember if she'd read or not. It didn't take her long before she had a stack of ten books to choose from.

Allie had a bad habit when picking a book off her to-be-read pile at home. She'd start reading without checking the title, and sometimes she'd read an entire book without knowing what it was called. Allie picked up the first book, read the back cover blurb, then the first couple of pages. She realized it sounded familiar to her, so she placed it back on the shelf where it belonged.

Allie repeated her process until she was down to just three books she hadn't read. Thinking that three books was one too many, and unable to decide which one to cut, she closed her eyes and shuffled the books as she counted aloud. Once she reached ten, she opened her eyes, removed the top book from the stack, and placed it on the shelf. Satisfied, she carried her two selections to the counter.

"Did you find what you wanted?" the bookseller asked as she approached. He was a short, rotund man, with hair swept over one side of his head to hide his bald spot. He wore gray slacks, a dark green dress shirt, and had a pair of reading glasses that dangled from a chain around his neck.

"Sure did," Allie answered. "Just some light bedtime reading for the week while I'm in town."

"I noticed you spent a lot of time in the history section. Did you not find anything to your liking?"

"To be honest, Mr…."

"Stanford Edison. You can call me Stan if you like."

"Okay. To be honest, Stan, I thought the books on local history and biography were a little overpriced for my liking. Sorry, I didn't mean to offend you if I did."

Allie expected Stan to get angry, but to her surprise, he just smiled at her. "Sorry, my dear. Most people who come in here don't even bother to check the price. They're more than happy to pay for whatever I ask, so why not get what I can for my books? It helps me keep the lights on."

"I understand," Allie said. "Trust me, if I lived here, I'd be in here all the time buying things, but I'm just here for some easy reads to get me through the week."

"If I may be so bold, perhaps I can interest you in this." Stanford reached to a stack of books behind him and handed one to Allie.

"*The Mystery of Quincy Bay*. What's this about?" Allie asked.

"It's part local history, part lore, part urban legend. It tells the story of a group of patriots who hide a treasure from the British during the early days of the revolution. According to local legend, the treasure is still out there, hidden in the area somewhere."

"Didn't Nicolas Cage make a movie about that?"

Stan smiled. "Well, similar concept, but this book is based on research done right here in Boston. It's more fact than fiction."

Allie flipped through the book. It was smaller in dimension than an average magazine, and she estimated it was fifty or sixty pages long. Inside, she saw several maps and photocopies of original source material, seemingly to support the printed text. She closed it, set it on the counter, and pointed at the author's names.

"S. Edison and H. Handon. Is S. Edison you?"
Stan grinned. "Yes. Hailey Handon is my co-author. She runs a local history museum not too far from here."

"Have you looked for the treasure yourself?"

"Oh, yes. Many times, in fact. The story has intrigued me since I first heard it as a little boy. Even now, when I get a day to myself, I chase down leads. I'll find it someday, I'm certain of it."

Allie thought about it for a second, then pushed the book forward. "No, thanks. Lost treasure stories aren't really my thing."

Stan pushed it back toward her. "Trust me. With all the local history in here, you'll love the book, even without the treasure aspect of it. Besides, it's only ten dollars."

Allie shook her head. "No. But thank you. I'll just take these two paperbacks."

Stan took the books from her and rang them in on his register. "How about five dollars? Come on, you'd be helping an independent author."

Allie gave him a deep sigh. "Okay, five dollars, but you'll have to sign it for me."

"Excellent," Stan said. He grinned as he found a pen, opened the front cover, and signed his name in a large, fancy script. As he did so, Allie dug a ten-dollar bill from her wallet and placed it on the counter.

"That will come to nine twenty-five," Stan said as he took the ten and replaced it with three quarters. As he placed her books into a plastic bag, Allie slid the coins into her pocket.

"Thank you," Allie said.

"No, thank YOU," Stan responded. "If you have questions about that book, any at all, I'd be happy to talk with you about them. You can stop by in person while you're in town. Or, if you prefer, contact me via phone or email on the bookmark I put in your bag."

Allie smiled and did a hasty exit from the shop. She gave a large exhale, thought about going back to the hotel, changed her mind and jaywalked across the street to the Boston Common. There, she found a bench in the sun, took out one of her new paperbacks and turned to the first page.

CHAPTER FIVE

"Allie? Hey, Allie?"

Allie opened her eyes, and it surprised her to see Drake standing over her with a concerned expression on his face.

"What are you doing here?" she asked. She looked around, confused at first, then she realized she'd fallen asleep. Napping was something she often did when she read in her backyard at home. She looked down at the book she was still holding in her cramped hand. She'd made it all the way to page four.

"I called you. Several times, in fact, so I got worried and came out looking for you."

"How did you find me?"

Drake held up his phone. "Location sharing. Remember?"

"Oh, yeah. Sure. The Great Kentucky Incident of 2020."

A few years earlier, they had been out in a geocaching road rally and had become separated. The group Allie was traveling with forgot about the rally all together and instead took a tour of the local bourbon distilleries. She lost cell service and could not call Drake to come and save her. Eventually, a worker at the third distillery she entered took pity on her and let her use the shop's phone to call out. After that experience, Allie and Drake agreed to download a location sharing app on each of their phones so they could find each other if one of them ever turned up missing again.

Allie dug her phone out of the back pocket of her jeans and checked it. She saw the seven missed calls from Drake, then turned the ringer up. "Sorry. I had it on silent."

"No worries. Geneva called. She's going to be a little later than projected, but recommended we head over to the restaurant to get a table. It's a popular place."

"Where are we going?"

"For Mexican food. Are you hungry?"

At the thought of a burrito, her stomach rumbled. "Yes. I suppose I could eat. Is the restaurant walkable from here, or do we need to catch a cab?"

Drake checked the map app on his phone, found the restaurant, and determined the distance from the bench to the front door. "It's about a half mile from here."

"Alrighty, mister, let's go." Allie got up from the bench, stretched, and followed Drake.

"How was your nap?" Allie asked.

Drake rubbed the back of his neck and turned sideways to avoid a woman pushing a stroller toward him. "It was good. I didn't even intend to take a nap. I wanted to rest my legs for a while. You were right to not climb that tower. My calves are still stinging!"

Allie chuckled. "That's what you get for being a nut. We're on vacation here. Let's try to take it easier for the rest of the trip."

"Sounds good to me."

They walked in silence the rest of the way to the restaurant, and once they arrived, the host escorted them to a table right away. The server dropped off menus, glasses of water, a bowl filled with tortilla chips, and individual bowls of salsa for each of them.

"I discovered the coolest little bookstore," Allie said as she dunked a chip into the salsa and ate it. "The guy there sold me the oddest thing."

Allie dipped into her bag and passed the book over to Drake. "According to the owner, who is also the writer of this book, there's a secret buried treasure out there somewhere."

"Who buried it? Pirates? You realize that's only an old wives' tale. Pirates never buried their treasure, and now that I think about it, that makes little sense to me, anyway. Why would a pirate bury a treasure so far from home? That would be like us putting our money in a local bank in Denver instead of Nashville."

"He claims the patriots did it to hide it from the British," Allie said.

"Isn't that the plot of some old movie?"

Allie laughed. "That was the same thing I said, except I didn't remember the name of the movie."

Drake was about to pass the book back when someone appeared at the table.

"Can I take your order?"

Allie looked up and grinned. "Ingrid! I'd forgotten Geneva told me you'd be joining us for dinner!" Allie jumped up from the booth and took Ingrid into a big embrace.

"You forgot? How would you forget about me? I'm hurt," Ingrid teased.

"How have you been? I haven't talked to you in forever," Allie said.

"I've been good. Sorry, I've been busy with final grades at school. Those are always a nightmare for me, and they're even worse now."

A server dropped off a glass of water for Ingrid and refilled the glasses for Drake and Allie.

"Why is that?" Allie asked.

"I have a two-part final exam in my classes. The first part is a test with questions that span what I taught in class for the entire school year. It's multiple choice, so it's not that bad. The horrible part is I also ask students to submit a thousand-word term paper with references. Apparently, it's vogue now to ask the artificial intelligence programs on the Internet to write the paper for you. I had to fail a quarter of the class for plagiarism."

"No way," Allie said, shocked. "How did you catch them?"

Ingrid smiled. "It's easy when half of my students are too lazy to change anything that comes out of the computer. I must have had a dozen copies of the same essay, right down to the title and footnotes. Next, I always check the word count. Typically, the word count won't come in exactly at a thousand. Sometimes it's nine-eighty, or, more commonly, is over by a few sentences. Students often think that adding an extra hundred words will get them on my good side. Those dozen copies, and several others, had exactly a thousand words. No more, and no less. After that, it was a matter of checking the phrasing and the voice, you understand. These kids have been writing papers for me all year, so I can tell at this point who sounds authentic, and who doesn't."

"That's too bad. I always enjoyed writing essays in school," Allie said.

"You would," Drake teased. Drake, not really a part of the conversation, had the book open in front of him, and went back to scanning through the material.

"I suspect you'll have a lot of angry students and parents," Allie continued.

Ingrid shrugged. "All my students understand the

consequences of cheating. It's right there in the class rules, and they all must sign an ethics pledge at the beginning of the year. I'm thinking of getting out of teaching, anyway. Too many headaches for too little pay."

Allie nodded. She couldn't blame Ingrid for that one bit.

"Anyway, enough of that. What did you do today?" Ingrid asked.

"After Geneva picked us up from the airport, she took us to a multi-cache out in Lexington."

"The one at the old taverns? Where the final is the birdhouse in the woods?" Ingrid asked.

"Yep. That's the one. Afterwards we went and explored the USS *Constitution*, and after that, we visited Bunker Hill."

"Did you climb the monument?"

Allie shook her head. "Not with my knee. He did, though." She had a chip in her hand and pointed it in Drake's direction. She had a bit of salsa on it, which dripped back into the bowl.

"How was that for you, Drake?" Ingrid asked.

"It was fine," Drake answered without looking up from the book.

Allie laughed. "Fine. Sure. Afterwards Geneva and I practically had to carry him back to the car, and he had to take a nap."

Ingrid joined in on the laughter. "That sounds exactly like what happened to me. I didn't walk right for three days after making that climb. I'm never doing that again."

"Join the club," Drake murmured.

"You're looking super good. You cut your hair." Allie said.

"How could you notice? We haven't seen each other in almost a year, and I only took off about an inch." Ingrid ran her fingers through her hair that barely touched her shoulders. It was so blond it almost looked white. She was a Danish beauty, with ice-blue eyes and alabaster skin that was just beginning to tan with the help of the early summer sun.   "Enough about me. How are you? Are you back to teaching your full slate of classes? The last time we talked, you weren't."

Allie shook her head. "Not yet. I'm still only doing water aerobics. It'll be another couple of months before I start on anything more strenuous."

Ingrid frowned. "I'm sorry."

Allie patted Ingrid's hand. "No need to be sorry. It was my own carelessness that caused it to happen."

"Are you ready to order?" the server asked as she approached the table, order pad in hand.

"I'm sorry. We're still waiting for one more person. She should be here soon," Allie said. "Won't she Drake?"

The server turned her attention to another table.

"Drake? Hello?"

"Hmm. Oh, sorry. I didn't mean to ignore you. This book is fascinating. I wonder if this is actually real."

"What book?" Ingrid asked.

Drake closed it and passed it across the table. Ingrid set her water glass aside to make room and opened the book on the table and started paging through it. After a few minutes, she closed the book and handed it back to Drake.

"I've heard of this treasure before, but it's not always referring to Quincy Bay. Sometimes it's Broad Sound, or Mystic River, or Dorchester Bay. Regardless, the story is mostly the same. During the revolution, a group put together a big treasure that was buried somewhere. So far as I know, no one has ever come close to proving anything other than it's simply a story."

"Yeah, but look at these," Drake said as he flipped the book open to a picture of a handwritten letter. As with most letters of that age, the script was difficult to read.

Ingrid shrugged. "Yeah, so? I saw a photograph once of the Loch Ness Monster, but no one has ever proved it's really in that lake, either."

"Okay, that's a valid point," Drake said. He held the book across the table for Allie to take, but she waved him off.

"You can keep that if you're interested. I only bought it to get away from the guy," Allie said.

Drake took the book and set it down on the floor, leaning it against the chair leg.

"I wish Geneva was here so we could eat," Drake said as he pulled another chip from the basket.

"Wish granted, sweetie pie," Geneva said as she appeared as if from out of thin air. She leaned over and gave Drake a kiss and moved to her chair.

Allie and Ingrid looked at each other and giggled. "Get a room," they teased in unison.

Geneva picked up her menu and swatted Ingrid with it, then looked at it, turned it right-side up, and looked at it again. "Did you order yet?"

"Nope. We were waiting for you," Ingrid said.

"Do you at least know what you want?" Geneva asked as she drummed her fingers on the table as she read through the menu.

"Steak fajitas," Drake said.

"Shrimp tacos," Allie answered.

"I'm having the beef enchiladas with Mexican rice. No beans. She's having the classic burrito with sour cream and guacamole on the side," Ingrid said.

"How did you guess that?" Geneva asked.

Ingrid smiled and reached for a chip. "We've been here a dozen times, and you always get the same thing."

"Will there be anything else? Anything besides water to

drink?" the server asked, jotting the last of the order down.

Allie ordered a Diet Coke, while the other three opted for frozen strawberry margaritas.

Geneva had a smile on her face the size of a Ford Bronco, but everyone stared at her without saying a word for a good while.

"Okay, I'll get it going," Drake said. "How was your day, honey?"

Geneva excitedly clapped four times, loud enough to attract glances from the surrounding tables. "It's official! I'm conducting the symphony on Friday! Look, I'm sorry it took so long for me to get here, but I had to work over arrangements, timing, and material and I had to figure out what to do with the cello chairs. I'm so excited!"

"I'd be excited too, conducting for the world-famous Boston Symphony," Allie said.

Geneva smiled, and her cheeks blushed. "It's not the Boston Symphony, Allie. I thought you guys knew that. I'm with the Boston Common Symphony. We do shows throughout the summer in the Boston Common park. Under the stars, it's really quite nice."

"It sounds nice," Allie said. "I didn't mean to offend you, and I'm sorry if I did."

Geneva dismissed her with a wave of the hand. "You didn't. Sure, it's not as prestigious, but that doesn't mean the musicians aren't any less talented. Besides, the whole idea of our symphony is to bring the classics to the people in a new way, and since it's in the park, it's more relaxing and much more fun."

"I'm looking forward to it," Drake said. "Are you sure you're going to be ready? Friday is only a couple of days away."

Geneva waved him off, too. "Of course. I was already the second backup for the conductor anyway, so I was in on all the show planning from the beginning."

Drake looked up and saw the server approaching with plates in hand, followed by a second server. Once they passed out all the meals, Drake picked up his glass to toast. "Here's to a great week with great friends."

Everyone touched glasses, took a sip, then turned their attention to their meals. Drake settled in as he usually did, which was like an underfed wild hyena that hadn't eaten in weeks. Even though he had to assemble his fajitas, he did so quickly. Then he ate them with haste, as though he expected someone to swoop in and take his fork and his plate away from him. He could eat slower, and did so when occasion dictated him to, like at special occasion dinners like weddings, but for the most part, he inhaled his food.

Ingrid almost gave him a run for the money. She had three enchiladas on her plate resting on a bed of Mexican rice. Ingrid used her spoon to cover her enchiladas with additional salsa from her bowl, then used the same spoon to cut off an end of one enchilada and eat it. She looked up and saw Allie watching her. "What?"

Allie took a drink of her Diet Coke to knock down the chunk of taco she'd just eaten, then cleared her throat. "I noticed in Arizona, but I didn't ask then. Why do you eat everything with a spoon?"

Ingrid swallowed, then held her spoon out before her. "Because. The spoon is the perfect utensil. All you need to do is scoop and eat. You can eat anything with a spoon. You can't say the same of a fork. Can you eat soup with a fork? No. The spoon is superior. There isn't anything you can't eat with a spoon."

"What about spaghetti?" Drake asked. "You can't eat any noodle dish with a spoon."

"You can if you cut them up first," Ingrid argued.

"And just exactly how do you use a spoon and knife rather than a fork and knife?" Drake asked.

Ingrid showed everyone by pushing down on the top of her enchilada with her spoon and slicing off a piece with her knife. "Tah-dah!"

Drake shook his head, rolled his eyes, and returned to vacuuming his meal.

"Why aren't you two eating?" Ingrid asked as she pointed her spoon in Allie and Geneva's direction.

The women looked down at their plates. While Drake was a bite away from finishing, and Ingrid had but one enchilada to finish, the burrito and shrimp tacos had barely moved. Allie and Geneva looked at each other, silently sharing the secret of the late afternoon ice cream treat, then at Ingrid.

"Too many chips?" Allie said.

Geneva nodded enthusiastically. "Yes! Too many chips. And I'm really excited about the symphony, and my adrenaline hasn't calmed down yet, so I'm sure I'll be hungry any time now."

Ingrid was suspicious, but she let it drop and concentrated on her own meal. "So, what's the plan for after dinner?"

"Good question. Actually, maybe the four of us can go back to the hotel and play cards all night. The four of us. All night long," Allie said.

Drake's attention was on something across the room, but he turned and focused in on Allie long enough to pass her a dirty look.

Ingrid saw Drake's evil eye and doubled down to further antagonize him. "You know what would be even better? A nice long game of Monopoly. Four is the perfect number of players. Why, I bet the game would last until breakfast. Lunch, perhaps."

Drake expelled a loud sigh that was meant only for his

inside voice, then coughed quickly to cover it up. Geneva didn't say a word. She just sat back in her chair and enjoyed the entertainment.

"Actually, you know what, Ingrid? I haven't been to the movies in a long time. Do you know if there's a theater around here?" Allie said.

"There's one about three blocks from this restaurant," Ingrid answered. "It's got just short of a million screens."

"What do you say you and I go over there after dinner? I'm sure there's a nice chick-flick we can see."

Ingrid wrinkled her nose. "Ack. I'm more of an action or sci-fi kind of girl."

Allie's countenance brightened. "Even better. I don't really like chick-flicks either. Or anything that would cause me to cry. If I wanted to cry out in public, I'd stand on the corner and check my bank balance."

Everyone at the table laughed.

"So, what do you say? Want to go on a movie date with me, Ingrid?"

She nodded. "I do. Provided we can get some popcorn with extra butter. And as long as these two sticks in the mud don't come along. I couldn't stand to hear another word about the symphony."

"And if I have to suffer through another word about Drake's aching legs, I think I'll throw up. Nope, it's just you and I tonight," Allie said.

Allie looked over at Drake. He mouthed some words, and although she couldn't hear them, she knew what they were. Thank you.

CHAPTER SIX

The group arrived at Paul Revere's house twenty minutes before it opened after almost a mile hike from the hotel. Drake and Geneva took the lead on the walk since Geneva knew the area well and could get there without a map. Not that they needed a map, since once they got on the Freedom Trail, all they had to do was follow the familiar red bricks. However, Geneva also showed them a couple of shortcuts, which saved some walking time for them all.

"There's a virtual cache here," Geneva said as she slid her sunglasses up onto her head. "It's a fairly easy one. When the building opens, we can go in and glance around."

Drake opened the geocaching app on his phone and searched for the cache. When he found the correct one, he read off the description. "Take a picture in front of the building and provide the count of the number of stones in the foundation beneath the door. That seems simple enough. What can go wrong? It's only a virtual."

Allie snickered. "Are you kidding? Plenty can go wrong. Remember that time we were trying to find the answers to the questions at that war memorial by that county courthouse? The one where the police stopped us and questioned us?"

"Really? What happened?" Geneva asked.

Drake rolled his eyes. "It wasn't anything major. The local sheriff caught us scouring the war memorial for information and wanted to find out what we were doing."

"You forgot to mention it was the middle of the night, and he thought we were terrorists intent on blowing up the courthouse," Allie said.

"Okay, okay," Drake said. "We were coming back from a geocaching event in Alabama—"

"It was in Georgia," Allie interrupted.

"Come on, Allie, I'm trying to tell the story. Like I said, we were coming back from an event in Georgia. Allie was driving, and I was looking for nearby caches and spotted this virtual cache coming up. It seemed easy enough, find a few names on the war memorial and send them to the cache owner to get the credit. No big deal. We get to the courthouse at just after sunset—"

"It was one in the morning, Drake," Allie said. "Right after sunset? You need to get your memory checked."

Drake threw Allie a glare and continued. "We arrived at a few minutes after one in the morning. Because it was night out, I got out my flashlight and headed to the dimly lit memorial and started looking for names. Little did we know, the police station was right across the street. Apparently, the town's sheriff noticed us and wandered across the street to see what we were up to. No big deal."

"Is he missing any other important details, Allie?" Ingrid asked.

Allie smiled. "Only the part where neither one of us spotted the sheriff coming across the street toward us. Drake had found a name and was writing it down in his notebook when a light bright enough to use in a lighthouse appeared and the sheriff yelled 'freeze'. Drake dropped his notebook and pen and froze.

Me being me, I started laughing so hard, the gum I was chewing flew out of my mouth and landed smack dab on the sheriff's right boot."

"That didn't happen," Geneva said. She glanced at Drake, who raised an eyebrow and nodded.

"What happened next?" Ingrid asked.

"Same thing that always happens when we encounter a LEO," Drake said.

"What's a LEO?" Ingrid asked.

"Law enforcement officer," Allie answered. "We explained what we were doing there and what geocaching is. The sheriff had never heard of it before and thought we were there to vandalize the monument. Then backup showed up, and fortunately, the deputy who arrived was also a geocacher. Once she validated everything we said, we were off the hook."

"Only after Allie retrieved her gum from the man's boot," Drake said.

"He wanted to cite me for littering, but didn't," Allie said. "Crisis averted. After that adventure, we found the last couple of names we needed. We logged the cache and rolled out of town, never to return."

"Can we end it with the stories and do this thing?" Drake asked.

Drake turned around and looked at the building. The two-story wood house looked out of place in its environment. It was well-maintained, with a coat of dark gray paint, clean windows, and all the shingles on the roof lined up perfectly and seemed accounted for. Even though it was immaculate, it looked alien abutted against a coffee shop, and dwarfed by the four-story buildings in the surrounding area.

"Take our picture?" Drake asked of Geneva.

Geneva nodded, and Drake handed her his phone, and grabbed Allie to get into the frame. Together they gave a thumbs up as Geneva snapped the photo. The picture part was complete, so Geneva and Ingrid walked across the street. There, they found a small, three-foot high wall surrounding the parking lot of another building, so Geneva and Ingrid sat. While the women rested, Drake and Allie counted the stones and joined their friends.

"Ten." Geneva said as Drake sat down next to her. He took his backpack off and put it on the ground next to his feet.

"We were arguing if it was nine or ten. We're not sure whether to count that real little one," Drake said.

"It's ten. We disagreed about it, too. I logged nine when I answered the question, but the cache owner messaged me that the answer was incorrect and urged me to try again. So, go with ten."

Drake continued to work, logging the find for the geocache. Once complete, he sent the photo to Allie so she could do the same. He stretched his legs out in front of him and took Geneva's hand. "I feel like it's going to be an interesting day filled with fun and wonder."

"That's a goofy thing to say," Geneva teased.

"I'm a goofy guy. Hey, did we drive by this place yesterday?" Drake asked.

Geneva reached over and took Drake's hand in hers. "No, why?"

"I think I've seen this building before."

"You probably noticed it in some travel brochures. It's not uncommon to recognize pictures of it in this town."

"Yeah, I suppose you're right. There's a mural of Freedom Trail locations on a wall in the hotel lobby. I probably spotted it there." Drake gave Geneva's hand a gentle squeeze. He felt so good being so close to her.

A half-dozen tourists lined up to enter the house, and Ingrid and Allie stood intending to join the queue. Allie stretched and put her backpack on her shoulders.

"You two coming?" Ingrid asked.

"Hold on a second," Drake said. He grabbed his backpack, unzipped it, and pulled out the book Allie gave him. He flipped through the pages and stopped when he came to the photo of the house. "See, I knew I saw it somewhere."

"What does it say?" Geneva asked.

Drake scanned the text, turned the page, and flipped back. "Not much. Only speculation that Paul Revere was one of the few people who knew the location of the treasure. According to the book, the secret to the find lies inside the house. Is this really his house?"

Geneva shrugged. "I think so, but I've never been inside, so I couldn't tell you for sure."

Drake stowed the book back into the backpack and returned the pack to his shoulders. "Let's go. We'll see if there's anything to see. Perhaps we'll get lucky and there will be an unattended treasure map inside, complete with GPS coordinates and an X to mark the spot."

The four queued up and waited to enter the building. Once they got inside, Drake spotted a tour guide and walked over and said hello.

"Is this the original building where Revere lived?" Drake asked.

The guide handed Drake a brochure. "The building itself is about ninety percent original. There are some furniture and personal items that are from the Revere family. Of course, there are several reproductions and other original period pieces that didn't belong to the Reveres."

Drake took the pamphlet, glanced at it, then shoved it in his back pocket. "Thanks."

They wandered around the house at their own speeds. Drake, who wasn't as interested in the history behind things, rambled around, giving only casual glances at items as they passed through the house. To her credit, Geneva stayed by his side the entire time.

Allie, who was a history buff, lingered in each room, and stopped to inspect every item in each room, regardless of the room's purpose. When she and Ingrid got to the kitchen, they found Drake and Geneva standing in front of the gigantic fireplace that dominated the room.

"All these cool things, and you're concentrating on the fireplace?" Allie asked when she got to them.

Without looking at her, Drake spoke. "The fire of revolution starts in the home's hearth."

"Huh?" Allie asked.

"There. Above the fireplace."

Allie's eyes went from the fireplace to above it. On the mantle there were several items, including bellows, what looked to be a small butter churn, and a few silver plates on display. Above them all, attached to the wall, was a needlepoint featuring the words Drake had just read.

"I'll be right back." Drake left the three women standing there and disappeared from the room.

"That was odd," Allie said, "even for him."

A few moments later, Drake reappeared with the tour guide in tow. He pointed to the embroidery. "What can you tell us about that?"

The tour guide smiled. "Ah, good eye. Can you guess how often I get asked about that piece? Once or twice a year at most. We can trace that embroidery back to Rachel Revere, Paul's second wife. The story goes that as the talk of revolution warmed up, Paul had her create that embroidery to remind them of the time they lived in."

"Wow, that's been hanging on that wall for almost two-hundred and fifty years?" Allie asked.

"Not quite. The Reveres took it with them when they sold the house in 1800. When Revere's great-grandson got this house, he returned the piece to that spot above the mantle where it's hung since the early 1900s. Other than being cleaned and framed for its protection, it's hanging like it was back then. Sadly, that artwork is probably one of the most overlooked and under-appreciated items in the entire house."

"Thank you. That was a great story," Drake said. The guide nodded at the group and then stepped away.

"You've got that look in your eye, Drake. What are you thinking?" Allie asked.

"I'm thinking, since we're here anyway, we should check out this fireplace and determine if there's anything odd about it."

"Are you saying there's a hidden compartment in the fireplace, like that one at Cacheland?" Geneva said. "If you are, we certainly can't go looking for it. There are security cameras in this room, and I doubt they would catch us on the monitor and continue to let us tear apart a piece of American history."

"No. I'm not saying that at all. No need to touch. Just use our eyes."

The four spread out to the width of the fireplace and examined the entire thing. After a few minutes, Drake stepped away. "This isn't working. We've got too many chefs in the fire, and we're just getting in each other's way."

"Why don't Allie and I go check the one upstairs?" Ingrid said. "You two give this one a thorough searching. If we have found nothing in, let's say, ten minutes, we'll swap fireplaces. If we still can't find anything, then we just need to agree that there's nothing to be found and go on about our day, okay?"

"I think that's a good idea," Allie said. "After all, there's zero chance that there's something here to be found after all this time."

Drake considered it for a moment, then relented. "Okay. Sounds like a plan to me."

Allie and Ingrid left the room, leaving Drake and Geneva to search the ground floor fireplace on their own. They spread out, and each took a side of the fireplace that stood four feet tall and eight feet wide.

Drake started with the topmost brick in the firebox and scanned each one in the row, and once he got to the end, he moved on to the second row. He continued his methodical search until he finished the last row, then did the same with the back of the fireplace. There was a cutout that looked like a 1700s version of a pizza oven, and a cutout below that held firewood. Unlike a modern-day fireplace, the bricks weren't perfectly flush with each other. That construction caused nooks, crannies, and depressions that he couldn't closely examine. In places, the bricks jutted out slightly, which caused shadows to cover other bricks, making some areas impossible to investigate.

Besides the bricks, the fireplace also had items in it. There was an iron grate holding a small pyramid of wood, and a long bar which spanned the length of the fireplace. From the bar, a kettle and a cast iron cooking pot hung on hooks, making it impossible for Drake to examine the bricks behind them.

"Any luck?" Drake asked Geneva.

"Nope. The only thing I see are the strange looks we're getting from other people who enter the room. They probably think we're nutty."

"Maybe we should switch sides," Drake offered.

Geneva agreed, so they changed positions. Drake started his search all over again, except this time he felt even less likely he'd locate something. He trusted that if there was something to find where he was looking, Geneva would have found it already. After another five minutes of staring at stones, Drake stepped back and shook his head.

"Maybe we should swap with Ingrid and Allie," Geneva said.

Drake opened his mouth to answer, but before he could say anything, Allie entered the room and grabbed him by the shirtsleeve. "Come on, let's go. I'm bored. Ingrid's already outside waiting for us."

Drake let his mouth hang open for a moment, then closed it

and allowed himself to be led from the house. As they exited, they spotted Ingrid sitting on the wall where they had rested earlier.

"Did you show them?" Ingrid asked.

"Show us what?" Geneva said.

Allie pulled her phone from her pocket, sat down, and opened the photo gallery. She passed the phone to Drake. "Take a gander at that."

Drake looked at the phone. It showed a firebox that looked similar, but not exactly the same, to the one he'd spent several minutes staring into.

"The upstairs fireplace?" he asked.

"Yep. Swipe to the next picture."

Drake did as ordered. There was a closeup area of three bricks in particular.

"What do you see?" Allie asked.

Drake shrugged. "Soot?"

Allie took her phone back and expanded the photo. "Ingrid spotted it. She's the hero. Look again."

Drake took the phone back, and with Geneva looking over his arm, he spotted what looked like letters crudely scratched into the brick. "Are these initials? Looks like an L, a V with a dot in it, and a backward C. Who is LVC?"

"Could have been anyone," Geneva said. "The brick maker? The guy who built the fireplace? A random piece of graffiti?"

"That's what I figured too, but the dot was bothering me. That's when I realized it was pigpen cipher, also known as a Freemason's cipher," Allie said.

"Paul Revere was a Freemason," Ingrid added.

"In pigpen, the first L would be a C, the V with the dot would be a W, and the backward C would be a D. CWD," Allie said.

Drake handed the phone back. "Okay. So, we're back to three initials. CWD? Who's CWD?"

"Why go through the trouble of a cipher for just initials? What if the C wasn't the letter, but see as in look? Like go see WD."

"Makes sense," Drake said, "but how to you know which WD would be associated with Paul Revere?"

Ingrid smiled and raised her hand. "I know that one. William Dawes. He was on the ride with Revere that night."

"You sure?" Drake asked.

Allie put her hands on her hips. "Of course, she's right. We were just at his capture site yesterday. Don't you remember reading the signs?"

Drake grinned.

"I'll take that as a no. Clearly, we're meant to go find William Dawes. Anyone know anything about him?"

Ingrid used her phone to find some information. "He was born in Boston, baptized at the Old South Church, and was a tanner, did the midnight ride and became a major in the militia. Any of this helpful?"

Drake and Allie looked at each other. "Not really. When did he die?"

"In 1799. Said to have been buried in King's Chapel Burying Ground, but then now they think he's buried in Jamaica Plain." Ingrid looked up from her phone and saw the blank faces looking back at her. "We're not getting anywhere with this, are we?"

Drake, Allie, and Geneva shook their heads in unison.

"Any chance his house is a tourist attraction?" Geneva asked.

Ingrid went back to her phone. "Says here he lived at 64 Ann Street. I wonder where that is." Ingrid clicked at the keys for several more minutes until she spoke. "Okay. Got it. Ann Street doesn't exist anymore, but now it would be at around 6 North, which is about a half mile from here back near Faneuil Hall. Should we go?"

Drake smiled. "Why not? It's a beautiful day for a walk."

Ten minutes later, they arrived at the location.

"This doesn't look promising," Drake said as the four stood shoulder to shoulder, staring up at the plaque attached to the building about ten feet above them. According to the marker, William Dawes had a house at the location at one point. Where Dawes' house once stood was now a series of large red brick buildings that spanned the length of the entire block. The spot where William Dawes lived now nestled nicely in between a bank and a Korean restaurant.

"Well, now what?" Ingrid asked. "Is this the end of the road?"

Allie huffed, and her shoulders hunched. "I have an idea, but I don't really like it much."

Drake rubbed her back. "What is it?"

She looked up into his eyes. "I think we should take a trip to the bookstore."

CHAPTER SEVEN

The tiny brass bell above the door jingled as Allie entered the bookshop. The day before, the shop didn't seem all that small, but as Ingrid, Geneva, and Drake entered behind her, the space quickly filled up. Allie imagined with the skinny aisles it could accommodate only two more people inside before a line needed to form outside.

"You came back. And brought friends," Stan said when the group approached the counter.

"Yes," Allie said. She noticed right away he was wearing the same clothes as the day before. This morning, as she got closer to the man, she noticed an unpleasant smell about him. The stench reminded Allie of the odor stale fast food French fries left in the car after being closed up in the scorching sun all day.

"We're looking for information on William Dawes. Is there anything you can tell us?" Drake asked.

Stan was so fixated on Allie, he barely noticed that Drake and the others were there. It was only when Drake cleared his throat and repeated the question that Stan looked at him.

"William Dawes? The one who rode with Paul Revere?"

"Yeah, that's the one," Drake said.

"Hold on, let me check." Stan moved from the back of the counter and purposely bumped into Allie. On his way past her, gave her the creepiest smile she'd ever seen, and slipped into the aisle containing the local history.

"Drake, come up here," Allie yell-whispered.

Drake pushed his way past Geneva and Ingrid and switched places with Allie.

"You saw that, huh?" Allie asked in a quiet voice.

"Which part? The guy staring at your boobs, or trying to cop a feel?"

When Stan came around the corner, the smile dropped from his face when he noticed Allie was no longer standing where she had been. He approached the counter slowly. Rather than pushing his way through like he did on the way out, he excused himself and waited for Drake to step aside before he returned to his stool by the register.

"Well, did you find anything?" Allie asked.

"No. There were no books on Dawes himself. I checked a couple of local history volumes as well, but there was nothing in them you couldn't learn from the Internet."

"I guess we struck out," Drake said. "Let's go."

The four turned to leave. Geneva was now the first one in line, and she opened the door and stepped outside with Ingrid right on her heels.

"Wait!" Stan said. "If you still want to know more, go visit my colleague, Hailey Handon. She's the head of the Minuteman Museum, which is only a few blocks from here. She's also the co-author of the book I sold you. I can give you directions."

"What do you think?" Drake asked Allie.

"This is your quest. I'm up for it if you still are."

A few minutes later, as the group was walking down the street. Drake referred to the handwritten directions he'd received to make sure they were on the right path.

"The book guy was really creepy," Geneva said from out of nowhere.

"Yes, wasn't he?" Ingrid said. "I wouldn't worry, Gen, it seemed he only has eyes for Allie." Ingrid laughed and placed her hand on Allie's shoulder.

Allie playfully swatted Ingrid's hand away and huffed. "He certainly wasn't my type."

"Would you three knock it off? We're here," Drake said as he came to a stop.

Although the sign above the door proclaimed it to be the correct place, from the outside, it looked more like a dentist's office than a museum. The museum was in an ill-maintained red brick building. The front stoop had a chunk of concrete missing from the corner. In front of the building, the sidewalk had more pieces of litter on it than it had pedestrians walking by. The highlight was a black circle of spray paint on the wall where someone had covered some graffiti.

"You sure this is the right place?" Ingrid asked.

"It's the correct address, and there's that nice historical display in the window," Drake said.

In the window was the top half of a mannequin. Draped over its armless shoulders was the blue coat associated with the Continental Army, and on the head was the distinctive three-corner hat. Drake smiled when he noticed the soldier was wearing a Bruce Springsteen Born in the U.S.A. concert T-shirt under the coat.

"We're here. Might as well go in," Drake said. He stepped up two stairs and turned the doorknob, but it didn't open. Then he spotted a doorbell with a sign above it that read 'ring bell for entry'. The writing had letters so small, they could well have had a mouse write them. Drake pressed a button and heard a buzz inside. He waited for perhaps fifteen seconds, then pushed the doorbell again.

The door opened, and a woman's head appeared. Her

round face contained brown sparkling eyes, a button nose, chipmunk cheeks, and the most welcoming smile Drake had ever seen. She had her dirty-blond hair combed back and secured in a ponytail.

"Can I help you?" she asked.

"Um. We're here to see Hailey Hendon."

"That's Handon. Are you the folks from the bookshop?"

Drake nodded, and the woman threw open the door. "Well, come on in then. I'm Hailey. Stan called and said you'd be coming over. Said you wanted to know about William Dawes?"

Drake entered the museum and saw the body that accompanied Hailey's head. She was roughly six inches shorter than Drake, and she wore a pair of white capris pants, a teal t-shirt, and a pair of untied teal Converse shoes with no socks.

Before Drake could answer, a phone rang.

"I'd better get that. I'm expecting a call from the state archives. Please take a tour of the place while I'm gone," Hailey said.

Hailey flashed Drake another smile, then turned and walked down the hallway and disappeared behind a door marked private.

Drake turned around and bowed to the three women who hadn't even cleared the threshold of the door yet. "Come on in and have a look around."

Drake stepped past a small desk that acted as an entry point. There was a small wood donation box on the edge of the desk, surrounded by brochures for historic sites in the area, and a stack of bookmarks from Stan's bookshop.

Hailey had divided the museum into four main rooms, each one twelve-foot square. The first room they entered was the one that had the mannequin in the window. The featured piece was a diorama in the room's center that was four feet square and three feet high and featured the Battle of Lexington and Concord. Along the edge were descriptions of the troop movements and significant events of the battle, and next to each description was a red button.

As the resident history buff, Allie followed the entire perimeter of the diorama, read all the descriptions, and pushed all the red buttons. When a button got activated, a light would appear to direct your eye to that position in the diorama, but only roughly half of the buttons actually worked.

Considering it was a museum, Hailey had the rest of the first room furnished strangely. The display cases popular at jewelry stores lined most of the walls. Safely inside the cases were a mishmash of items. The treasures included coat buttons, clothing, musket balls, military supplies, and common household items. Overall, the room seemed more like a flea market than a museum.

The second room contained a diorama of the Battle of Bunker Hill. Like the first room, jewelry store cases lined the walls, but only half of them contained artifacts, and the others were empty.

The third and fourth rooms had no dioramas at all, and instead of display cases, file cabinets lined the walls, all of them locked.

It didn't take long for the quartet to make their way around the museum. They ended up back in the first room since it seemed to be the most spacious, well-lit, and least dreary of the four.

"Well, Allie, what do you think of the place?" Drake asked.

"Certainly not the most impressive museum I've been in," Allie answered.

"I know, and I apologize for that," Hailey said as she entered the room. "We're not much of a museum for physical artifacts as a repository for information related to the Revolutionary War."

"But the sign outside literally says Minuteman Museum," Ingrid argued.

Hailey's wide smile returned. "I know. I actually bought the building from the previous owner and since I liked the alliteration of the name, I kept it. The dioramas and the few artifacts we have were left over from him."

"So, you're not really a museum then?" Allie asked.

"No, but what I am is one of the most respected historians on the east coast. And only the Library of Congress rivals my collection of Revolutionary War documentation."

"My apologies, I didn't mean to offend you," Allie said.

"No apologies needed. It's a common mistake. It was my fault. I should have changed the name when I took over the place, but I didn't. Now so many people know of my work, I'm stuck with it. So, now, what can I do for you?"

"We're searching for information about William Dawes. Specifically, if there is anything around the area that is still here from when he was alive," Drake said.

"I'm not sure what you mean," Hailey admitted.

"For example, we toured Paul Revere's house this morning, then thought it would be fun to see where William Dawes lived."

"And you walked all the way there and found a Mexican restaurant and a donut shop?"

Allie smiled. "Donut shop is still there, but it's a Korean restaurant now."

"Really?" Hailey said. "I should go try that out. Anyway, as far as locations are concerned, the only things that come to mind are the Old South Church, where his parents baptized him, and his grave, of course. Other than that, there are a few monuments around, mostly dedicated to the ride. I'd have to check my archives on him."

"Would you mind? We're really interested."

Hailey hesitated, then agreed. "Okay, fine. Come along with me."

Hailey led the group into the fourth room, went directly to the third file cabinet on the east wall, and tugged at the second drawer from the top. Realizing she locked the files, she swore softly under her breath, then produced a single key from her pocket and unlocked the cabinet. As she slid open the correct drawer, Drake noticed a single small plastic golden retriever dangling from the keychain.

"What's your dog's name?" he asked.

"Daisy," she said without hesitating her search for the correct file.

"Ah, nice name," Drake said. His observation explained the short blond hairs on the back of Hailey's shirt.

"Here, take this." Hailey held out a three-inch-thick hanging file folder. Drake grabbed it and set it on top of the cabinet. Several manila folders and individual pages slid out, attempting to make as escape, so he put his hand on top of it to prevent anything from spilling onto the floor.

Hailey passed a second file folder to Drake, who handed it off to Allie. When Hailey found the third bundle, she stood up and closed the file drawer, and flashed an apologetic smile. "Sorry, but this is all I have on William Dawes. Come on, let's take these into the other room."

Drake gathered up his bundle, and everyone followed Hailey down the hallway and through the private door. One look around, and Drake believed they were in the room where all the action happened. It must have been a large storage and receiving room at one point because there was a large steel loading dock door on the north wall. Besides file cabinets, there were four aisles of makeshift shelving units. Altogether, Drake guessed, they held hundreds of books. In one corner were two old desks pushed together, on which there were enough newspapers stacked to provide each person in Boston their own copy.

The highlight of the room was two conference tables that were joined in the middle of the room to make one big table. There were five folding chairs around the table, and one leather rolling office chair. At one end of the table was a microfiche reader, and a small cart overflowing with reels of microfiche.

"Grab a chair, everyone," Hailey said. She made a beeline for the good one for herself. "Now, what are you looking for? Anything physically related to Dawes that might still stand today?"

"Yes, that's right," Drake said.

Hailey opened the folder in front of her and started dividing it into small stacks. "Okay, everyone, grab something from the pile and we'll see what we can see."

"Aren't you worried about us touching old documents?" Allie asked.

Hailey grabbed the first sheet off the top of the pile and held it up. "Not at all. These are all copies made from the originals. I keep all the source material in an off-site location for preservation, so don't worry about it. I'd die if I ruined a three-hundred-year-old ledger or something like that." She passed the piles around to everyone in the room, and they all got started looking through the documents.

Drake set the small stack of papers in front of him and squared the corners. The top page was a copy of Dawes' baptismal record, and since Drake knew the church was still standing, he set that aside. Letters Dawes had written to various people made up the next four sheets. Since they didn't mention any physical places, Drake turned them upside-down as he discounted them and stacked them neatly in their own pile. The last sheet he studied was a quartermaster's inventory of supplies with Dawes' signature on it. Since Drake didn't think the amount of turnips Dawes had on hand applied to his search, he added the sheet on top of the reject pile. Drake looked down and saw the only page he had was the initial one he found. As he surveyed the stacks of the others around the table, he saw they weren't faring much better.

Once they made their way through the first folder, Hailey took all the non-relevant documents and put them back. Then she divvied up the stack from the second folder and they repeated the process all over again. By the time they were through the third and final folder, they had around a dozen possibilities left before them.

"Okay, let's merge the notes," Hailey said. "What do you have?"

Drake started. "I've got the Old South Church. Anyone else have anything on that?"

Ingrid did, so she passed the page over to Drake, who set it with his sheet.

Geneva held up the only page she had. "I've got something related to the tannery he ran. There's an address mentioned here, but I can't read it." She passed the paper to Hailey, who studied it carefully.

Hailey's chair squeaked as she got up. She went to a bookshelf, ran a finger along the spines, then pulled out the book she was looking for and returned to the table. Hailey set the large atlas down and paged through it until she found what she wanted. She searched for the tannery's old location, then closed the book. "Nope. This is a park now. Quite a nice one down by the harbor. Next?"

"I've got a deed to his house, and a picture of his grave marker," Allie offered as she passed the papers forward.

"We all know the house doesn't exist anymore," Hailey said as she added that sheet to the discard pile. She held up the picture for all to see. "This marker is in King's Chapel Burying Ground, but it's speculated he's really buried with his first wife in Jamaica Plain."

"In New York?" Drake asked.

"No. It's a neighborhood in Boston, a couple of miles southwest of here. Anything else?"

"I've got some pictures of portraits," Allie said as she held them up.

"Ah, yes. Nice, aren't they? The portrait in your left hand is in Ohio. The other is in Illinois."

"Who's this?" Allie asked, setting down the papers she was holding and displaying a picture of a woman.

"That's a portrait of Mehitable May, Dawes' first wife. That's in Illinois as well."

"Last thing I have is this picture of a cannon," Allie said.

Hailey smiled. "Yes, of course. My favorite stories involving William Dawes weren't about the horse ride he took with Revere. Nope, it was his propensity for heisting cannons from the British that are my favorites. It's believed that is one of the many cannons he swiped. On the bottom of that page, it should tell you where they took the picture."

Allie turned the sheet around and looked. "Bunker Hill Museum." Allie passed the page to Hailey, who passed it to Drake.

"So here you are, everything that exists today related to William Dawes," Hailey said.

Drake spread out the items before him. A church, a grave marker, a cannon. Not much to go on.

"Hopefully, you have the answer you wanted?" Hailey asked.

"Not the one I wanted, but the one I got," Drake answered. He stood from the table and offered his hand. "Thank you for your time and the information. We really appreciate your help."

Hailey shook his hand. "No problem. That's what I'm here for. Come back anytime."

Drake nodded and ushered his friends from the room. They passed through the museum, out the door, and huddled together when they got to the street corner.

"Well, folks, what's the plan?" Allie asked.

"Where's the church from here?" Drake asked.

Geneva looked around to get her bearings. "Four or five blocks, I'd guess. Not far."

"And what about the cemetery?"

"A few blocks east of Boston Common."

Drake nodded. "Okay. Let's go check out the church, pick up Geneva's car from the hotel, then go to the cemetery and to the museum. Sound logical?"

Everyone agreed, and Geneva took Drake's hand and led him off toward the Old South Church.

CHAPTER EIGHT

"So, you have nothing here that would be from William Dawes?" Drake asked.

Drake waited for an answer. The pastor sitting behind the librarian's desk of the Old South Church library took off his reading glasses and placed them on the blotter.

"I'm sorry, son, but no. We have the records from back then in our off-site archives, but we have nothing else from that far back at this location."

Drake's eyes shifted from the pastor's eyes to the stained-glass window behind him. In it was the depiction of a blue summer sky, white clouds, and two doves sitting in a tree. Off on one side was a lone apple.

Drake readied himself to stand but settled back in his chair. "Wait, what do you mean by at this location?" Drake asked.

"True, this is the Old South Church, but this isn't the building that William Dawes and the rest of Boston used in the 1700s. They didn't build this church until 1837. If you want the physical location where Dawes worshipped, you want the Old

South Meeting House."

"Old South Meeting House?" Drake repeated.

"Yes, although before you go, you should know that the British practically gutted the interior during the war. Also, it almost burned down in 1872, but they restored it to its formal glory in 1877."

"Doesn't sound like I'll find what I'm searching for," Drake admitted.

The pastor shrugged. "Depends on what you're looking for. If you want to learn what life was like back in the beginning of the country, it's well worth a visit. Do you need directions?"

Drake shook his head. "No thanks. I'm visiting someone who's from here. And if she weren't around, I'll bet it's right on the Freedom Trail."

The pastor laughed. "That it is, son. That it is." He stood, shook Drake's hand, wished him well, and ushered him to the door.

"Well? What did he say?" Ingrid asked when Drake joined the others outside.

"He said we need to go to the Old South Meeting House. He said they built this church in the 1800s."

"That's my bad," Geneva said. "I should have realized that."

Drake took her hand, and they started walking toward the hotel. "Don't worry about it. It was a pleasant walk over here. Should we get your car and travel in style, or should we walk around all day?"

"With all the places we need to check, the car would be faster," Geneva said.

"And my knee's bothering me," Allie interjected.

Drake stopped, turned around, and looked at Allie. "Are you okay to get back to the hotel? Or we could get you a cab or an Uber."

"Or I could run ahead and get the car and pick you up here," Geneva said.

"How far is it to the hotel?" Allie asked.

"Less than half a mile," Geneva said. "We can cut through Copley Square. That would reduce some distance as well."

"Okay, I can make that." Allie said.

They maintained a slow, even pace to accommodate Allie's gait, and by the time they reached the hotel, she had a visible limp.

"Are you sure you don't want to rest for a while?" Drake asked Allie as Geneva retrieved the car from the parking garage.

Allie smiled at him. "I'll be good once I sit for a bit. I can do that in the car. Besides, what would you do without me? We both know I'm the brains of this operation."

Drake returned the smile without a word. When Geneva appeared, Drake opened the front passenger door and waited for Allie to take the seat. "You'll be more comfortable up front. Besides, I've been hoping for some alone time with Ingrid."

"I heard that!" Geneva yelled from the driver's seat. "And I've got a mirror here too, so I can keep my eye on you. Where to first?"

"Whichever one is closer."

"That would be the meeting house by about two blocks. Hold on, everyone."

Geneva didn't ease out into traffic as much as she bullied her way between cars that were waiting for the traffic light to change. She made two right turns and was finally satisfied she headed in the correct direction.

"I hope you two aren't too comfortable back there," she said as she glanced into the mirror.

Within a few minutes, the meeting house came into view.

Geneva bypassed it, continued on for two blocks and sat on her brakes while she waited for a guy in a white pickup truck to pull out. The second he left she swooped in to claim his spot.

"There's a no parking sign here," Drake said.

"Don't worry, it's for street sweeping. We're good until two in the morning. If we're here that long, we've got bigger problems than a traffic ticket," Geneva said. "Are you coming along, or do you want to stay here?" she asked Allie.

"I'm going to sit this one out," Allie said.

Geneva smiled. "I don't blame you. I'll leave you the keys so you can roll down the windows, or run the air, or listen to the radio. There are some non-aspirin pain relievers in the unmarked pill bottle in the center console if you want them."

"Good luck you guys," Allie said.

Drake, Geneva, and Ingrid got out of the car, and once they turned around, they immediately spotted the tall clock tower two blocks away. They covered the ground quickly, and within a couple minutes, they were standing outside the red brick building, looking up at the structure.

"It sure is impressive," Drake said. "To think that William Dawes was here once."

"As were Ben Franklin and Samuel Adams," Ingrid said.

"The beer guy?" Drake asked.

Geneva rolled her eyes and pulled Drake toward the entrance, and the three stepped into the building.

Drake expected to look at an ordinary church on the inside, and it surprised him when it was more than that. He stepped in far enough to get away from the door so others could enter and exit, and he stopped to glance around.

The color white dominated the interior. All around him, the walls, ceiling, railings of the second-floor balcony, window shutters, pulpit, and the pew backs were all painted white. The only other real splash of color was that of the stained wood that accented the top of the pew backs, the seats, and the well-worn floor. Along the outside walls there were several displays explaining the Boston Tea Party, along with other historical events from the time. The floor creaked beneath Drake's pacing feet as he studied the site.

Drake, Ingrid, and Geneva spread out and did a circle around the interior. Once they completed the ground floor, they followed the arrow downstairs. There, they discovered more exhibits and the obligatory gift shop. At the shop, they spotted the exterior door, stepped up a short flight of stairs, and found themselves outside the building.

"What do you think?" Geneva asked.

"I believe this stop was a waste of time. I discovered nothing to help us. Did you?" Drake said.

"No. Although there were a lot of places that were off limits to us. Should we go back in? Ask if we can get access to those areas?"

Drake shook his head. "No. Let's go over to the cemetery next."

They turned around and headed back to the car. A few minutes later they arrived and spotted Allie right where they had left her, windows down, her nose in a book. She finished the page she was on, inserted a bookmark, and stuffed it into her backpack. "How was it?"

"No luck. On to the next spot," Geneva said as she fired up the engine. She moved only a few blocks and found another space on the street to park her car. "It's about three blocks from here," she announced. She didn't bother to ask Allie if she was going along since Allie was already pulling the paperback from her bag.

They made quick work of the hike and found themselves at the main cemetery gate. Ingrid read aloud the signs attached to the fence listing the notable people buried before them.

"Too bad Allie's not here. She really enjoys visiting old cemeteries," Drake said. "Let's spread out and find the marker."

The three took different paths into the cemetery, and while Drake and Geneva headed off right away, Ingrid lingered and took a few photos with her phone. After she got some pictures she expected Allie would like, she strolled about five feet into the cemetery, then came to a stop. Before her was a square cement pillar, about three feet high, on which was placed a bronze plaque covered with a green patina. She took a picture, then read the inscription. "William Dawes Jr. Patriot, Son of Liberty, and first messenger sent by Warren from Boston to Lexington on the night of April 18-19, 1775 to warn Hancock and Adams of the coming of British troops. Born April 6 1745, died February 25 1799. Placed by the Massachusetts Society Sons of the Revolution April 19, 1899."

Ingrid looked to her side and discovered the person she'd felt approach a few seconds earlier was Geneva.

"I guess this is strike two," Geneva said. "He died well after the war was over."

Ingrid nodded in agreement. "Yeah. There isn't anything for us here. Where's Drake?"

Geneva spotted him in the far corner of the small cemetery, got his attention, and waved him over. "We rushed right past it," Geneva said when Drake got to their side.

Drake stopped for a second and read the inscription. "I guess this spot's a bust, too."

"That's what we felt as well," Geneva said.

"How did you guys make out?" Allie asked as the others climbed into the SUV.

"We had no luck there either," Drake said. "One last spot to try."

Geneva swerved in and out of stop-and-go traffic until finally, twenty minutes later, she spied a prime parking spot right in front of the museum. "Is this close enough for you?" she asked Allie as she undid her seatbelt and shut off the ignition.

Allie smiled and undid her belt as well. "I suppose I can make it that far. I have to use the restroom, anyway."

Geneva locked up the SUV, and the group filed into the museum. Allie made a beeline for the ladies' room, while the other three fanned out to search for the cannon. The museum wasn't a large one, and it didn't take long for Drake, Geneva, and Ingrid to meet up in the last room. There, they found the cannon. It was a small one, only four feet long and only a foot tall.

"Hailey said Dawes stole a cannon, and I didn't understand how he could," Drake said. "Of course, I was picturing those big guns we encountered on the *Constitution*. I didn't know they came mini-sized. I can understand how two men could easily pick this up and run away with it."

"Do you think Dawes handled this one?" Ingrid asked. "That's what the sign right there says. This cannon, rescued from the British by William Dawes, and so on," Drake said. "I was hoping we'd be able to get a good view of it, but clearly that's out of the question."

"Why?" Allie said as she entered the room.

Drake stepped aside so Allie could see what the rest of them did. The cannon, in its full glory, was covered by a glass display case to protect it from harm.

"Oh. I see," Allie said. "You can't see anything on it?"

Drake crouched and leaned in close enough for his breath to fog the glass. He examined as much of the cannon as he could, then stood. "I see nothing unusual. And of course, we won't see anything on the other side since it's pushed up against the wall."

Drake kneeled, inspected the cannon again, and came up

empty.

"I guess that's strike three. Game's over," Geneva said. "The game was fun while it lasted, though."

The four left the museum and stepped into the warm summer sun. Drake spotted the ice cream truck and jerked a thumb at it. "Who wants a treat? I'm buying."

Geneva and Allie looked at each other and laughed at the same time.

"What's so funny? What is it with you two?" Drake asked.

"Nothing," Allie said. "Get me a mint chocolate chip waffle cone, will you? I'll be over on the steps."

As Allie headed for the stairs, Ingrid gave her order to Geneva and rushed to Allie's side. While they waited, they both sat down in the shade.

Ingrid took out her phone, unlocked the screen, and offered Allie her phone. "Drake told me you like cemeteries, so I snapped some photos for you."

"Thanks, that's sweet of you," Allie said as she took the phone. She looked at the photos, then passed the phone back. "Looks like I missed the fun."

"You think cemeteries are fun?" Ingrid asked.

"I actually do. Just think about it. You stood a foot away from William Dawes' remains. Whenever I'm in that situation, I like to wonder about what that person's life was like, and how they got to be the person they were. I know it's silly, but hey, that's me."

Ingrid shook her head. "I don't figure that's silly at all. Besides, he wasn't really there."

Allie took a moment to brush a strand of hair over her ear. "What do you mean?"

"Remember what Hailey said? That they originally thought they buried him in that cemetery, but he's actually buried with his first wife? Or he was in that cemetery and then moved to be with the wife. I don't remember which."

"How many wives did he have?" Allie asked.

Ingrid shrugged, then looked for the answer on her phone. "Two. He was with his first for about twenty years, and the second he married after the first died."

"And he's buried with the first one? Where?"

"Forest Hills Cemetery in Jamaica Plain. In the May family plot."

"Sounds odd to me."

"What does?" Drake asked as he handed Allie her cone.

"We were just trying to figure out why they would bury Dawes in his first wife's family plot rather than with his second wife."

"I don't know, you tell me," Drake said as he licked from the side of his chocolate hazelnut cone.

"You know, I think I know where she's going with this. Are you thinking that we should check out his grave there?" Geneva asked.

"Yep, that's what I'm thinking."

"Well, let's go then," Drake said, taking a step toward the car.

"Whoa, there, tiger," Geneva said. "No ice cream in the car. Let's finish eating first and then continue the mission."

An hour later, Geneva pulled into the cemetery and parked next to the office. "I've been here before. The cemetery is huge, so I'm going to go in and see if I can get directions to where we're headed, and maybe a plot map."

Geneva left the car and stepped toward the building. She was about to walk up the stone steps to get to the office door when a small plastic box caught her attention. From inside, she pulled a map of the cemetery, glanced at it briefly, then carried it back to the car. She passed it over to Allie.

"Here's a map. I saw Dawes on there. Can you navigate us to the site?" Geneva asked.

"Of course. Give me a second to get my bearings." Allie studied the map for a moment. "Okay, I got it. Hey, did you know that E. E. Cummings and Eugene O'Neill are in here, too? Can we make a side stop?"

"After we're done with Dawes, we can make all the stops you like," Drake said.

"Yay!" Allie exclaimed with excitement. "Okay, go straight, then turn left at the third street you come to."
It wasn't long before they discovered the May family plot, with a small hill acting as a backdrop. They exited the car and approached the markers, ten of them lined up all in a row. Although some of the writing on some stones had been erased by nearly three hundred years' worth of sun, rain, wind, and snow, there was one that was easily read, a small, rectangle slab with the words "W. D. 1774".

"Is this the right one?" Allie asked.

"It can't be. Dawes didn't die until 1799," Ingrid said.

Drake shuffled from stone to stone, reading the names and dates that he could, then put his attention on the marker in the middle. "I agree. It seems odd, but let's check it out, anyway, okay?"

Drake approached the marker, crouched before it, and ran his fingers over the stone, as if some tactile impression would answer the questions he had in his mind. Besides the initials and the single date, there was no other information on the marker's front. Drake stood and walked to the back, crouched again, and examined the back. Again, he saw nothing but smooth stone. He lost his balance, and on instinct, he reached for the top of the stone to right himself.

He stood, then bent over, and looked at the stone's edge.

"Allie, come here a moment."

Allie made her way to the grave and when she arrived, Drake pointed at the top edge of the marker. "Run your hand along there. Feel any depressions?"

Allie rubbed the marker, then stopped. She looked around, found a small stick on the ground, and used it to clean the many decades' worth of debris from the stone. She wet her finger, then rubbed it over the spot. "It's an X."

She moved her fingers to the right, and an inch later came upon another depression.

"Hey Geneva, do you have any water in your car, and perhaps a towel I can use?" Allie asked. While Geneva went back to the SUV to look for the items, Allie used her stick and wet finger method to expose the next item. "E? Does that look like an E to you, Drake?"

Drake leaned over and looked. "Yeah, I think so. XE. Does that mean anything to you?"

"Not yet," Allie said, "but I'm hoping it will soon."

Geneva returned carrying a red shop towel, two bottles of water, and a toothbrush.

"I hope you're not going to want that back," Allie said.

Geneva laughed. "Of course not. I get them free from the dentist every time I go for a cleaning, so I must have two dozen of them under the bathroom sink at home."

Allie went to work on the stone. She used a gentle touch with the toothbrush to pick away at the debris, followed by a rinse and dry, and after several minutes of work, she finished.

"Anyone have a pencil?" Allie asked.

"Go ahead. I'll write it down on my phone," Ingrid said.

"Okay. N, G, G, H, P, X, F, E, R, F, G, F. Got it?"

Ingrid read the letters back to Allie, and Allie confirmed

they were correct.

"They make no sense to me," Geneva said.

Allie ran her fingers over the letters once more, then smiled. "Are you sure? You see these every single time you look at a hint on the geocaching website. It's a ROT13 Caesar cipher."

"I have an app to decode that," Geneva said.

"No need," Allie said. She stood up straight and pointed the toothbrush at the headstone. "It says Attucks rests."

CHAPTER NINE

"Attucks rests. Another riddle?" Drake asked.

"At least it's an obvious one," Ingrid said. "Historians believe Crispus Attucks was the first person killed in the Revolutionary War during the Boston Massacre."

"Does he have anything from the day? House? Gravestone?" Drake asked.

"I've never heard of him having a house in Boston, but I think there's a grave marker for him in the Granary Burying Ground," Geneva said.

"Good. Let's go there," Drake said.

Geneva took out her phone and checked the Internet for something, then shoved her phone back in her pocket. "We can't today. It closes at four, and we wouldn't make it there in time. Speaking of which, this place closes at four-thirty, and we promised Allie a visit to the other graves."

Allie nodded enthusiastically. "That's right, you promised. And you're not supposed to break a promise."

"You're right. Okay, everyone back in the car, and let's make this quick. I don't want to get locked in here for the night,"

Drake said.

Geneva grabbed Drake's arm and pulled him in close. "It's okay, darling. I'd protect you from the ghosts."

Drake laughed. "Thanks. I appreciate that. Let's get a move on. After this, I'd like to see if we can find something for dinner."

With Allie navigating, they searched the cemetery and found the last resting places of Cummings and O'Neill. At her insistence, they also stopped at several other interesting monuments as they drove past them. They realized it was time to leave when security caught up with them, reminded them of the time, and politely asked them to leave and return the next day if they wished.

Rather than fight the rush hour traffic back to the hotel, Geneva spotted a microbrewery with a restaurant a few blocks from the cemetery entrance. Although the parking lot was jam-packed with people who shared the 'it's five o'clock somewhere' mindset, Geneva found a spot for her SUV. Inside, they had a brief wait before they got a table for four in front of a large Plexiglas window. Behind the window were large stainless-steel vats and holding tanks. Above each of them were signs displaying the name of the beers being produced within.

Before long, Drake, Geneva, and Ingrid were sipping beers while Allie nursed a glass of water with lemon.

"What's the plan for tonight's activities?" Ingrid asked.

"I've got a rehearsal tonight at eight," Geneva said. "It's a run-through of Friday night's concert. You're welcome to come and sit in if you want to. It should only last a couple of hours, three at most."

"Don't most symphonies rehearse during the day?" Drake asked.

Geneva took a drink of her beer, a light apple ale, the specialty of the brewery. She smacked her lips, then took a second sip. "Oh, my, that's good. I have to remember this place exists and come here more often. Anyone got a pen?"

Allie had been playing with one of the brewery's heavy paperboard coasters. She had it standing on a corner beneath an index finger, then hitting it with the other finger and watching it spin. She stopped and handed the coaster to Geneva. "Here, take this home with you so you don't forget."

"Thanks." Geneva accepted the gift and shoved the coaster into her back pocket. "To answer your question, Drake, professional symphonies practice during the day. We're composed of mostly volunteers. We have benefactors and do fundraising to cover the expenses, and at the end of the year, any cash we've made above the budget gets split up among everyone. Although, it's rare someone will take the cash and run. Usually, we pool it and have a party, then roll the remainder to the next season. We're in it for the love of the music we play."

"Sounds nice. Would you mind if I joined you tonight?" Drake asked.

Ingrid and Allie passed a glance between them. Neither one seemed surprised that Drake wanted to go.

"Of course, I wouldn't mind. What about you two?"

"I think I'm going to rest up the knee," Allie said. "The hotel has a rooftop pool. Perhaps I'll hang out up there and read a book."

"I was going to go home, wash my hair, and watch television, but I guess I'll go hang out by the pool with Allie," Ingrid said.

Allie was in mid-drink, so she tipped her glass at Ingrid. "Come on over, you're more than welcome. What do you like to read?"

"Oh, you know, the classics. Like John Grisham."

"Sounds great. We can have a book club!" Allie exclaimed. She clapped a couple times, then leaned over, and gave Ingrid a high five.

Drake placed his hand on his forehead and shook his head. "Oh my. You two have a great time with that."

The group laughed, and soon they settled back down into casual conversation. A few minutes later, the server appeared with a tray filled with three burgers and a pulled pork sandwich for Geneva.

They were only half-finished eating when a man approached their table. Allie recognized his smell before he said a word.

"Hello, Stan, fancy meeting you here," Allie said without looking at him.

Stan stepped in closer to Allie, and in response, she leaned closer to Ingrid.

"You want to take a step back there, bud?" Drake ordered as he reached his arm out to shield everyone at the table. "What do you want?"

Stan shrugged. "I just wanted to see if Hailey gave you all the information you needed. She called me, you know, after you left her. Said you were interested in William Dawes. That's interesting. Is that why you were here at the cemetery? To see his grave?"

Drake was about to respond when Allie held up her hand and stopped him.

"Not that it's any of your business, but I was interested in Dawes because I love history. I learned all about the midnight ride, and never knew Revere wasn't the only one involved, so I wanted to know more about the others he rode with. You know all this. We asked you about it earlier, remember? And as far as our visit to the cemetery, I was there to see the graves of O'Neill and Cummings. As far as I know, they buried Dawes downtown. Now, if you'll excuse us, we have places to be later, so my friends and I need to finish dinner."

Stan sneered at her, then pulled away.

"Stan? One more thing," Allie said, her voice tempered with the sweetness of honey.

Stan turned back around and got close enough for Allie to

feel his breath on her neck.

"You've got ketchup on your shirt."

Stan stepped back, looked at his left sleeve, and finding nothing looked at his right. Sure enough, there was a bright red blob on his forearm. He took a napkin from the stack the server had left the group, wiped off the condiment, and dropped the napkin on the floor. He gave Allie a ghoulish smile, then turned and left.

"Odd coincidence seeing him here," Geneva said.

"Especially since his shop doesn't close until seven," Allie said.

"Do you think Hailey tipped him off on where we were going?" Geneva asked.

"I guess it's possible. Maybe he picked up our trail and followed us," Drake said.

"And what happens when he goes into that cemetery and finds the same code we did?" Allie asked.

Drake drained his beer and leaned back in his chair. "I'm not too worried. He'll be there, and we'll be a step ahead of him at the other cemetery. Also, you know I'm a stickler for the geocacher's code, right?"

The three women stared at him, each with a blank look on their face.

Drake smiled. "We're supposed to leave an area the same way we found it, right? He won't find those letters except by accident, the way I did, because I filled them all back in with mud, the exact way we found them. Anyone want another beer?"

*

The next morning, at five after nine, the four friends were in the Granary Burying Ground. They clustered in front of the granite memorial that marked the burial plot of Crispus Attucks.

"The remains of Crispus Attucks, victim of the Boston Massacre, March 5th, 1770, were here interred," Allie read. "Well, here he is."

"Not what we need, though. It's the last line that bothers me," Drake said. "Placed by Boston Chapter S.A.R. 1906. 1906. The marker's not original."

"I guess we need to find something else related to him. What about where the Boston Massacre took place?" Allie asked.

Geneva shook her head. "No. There's a historical marker embedded in the ground there, nothing else. I've walked past it myself like a hundred times."

"Do you guys mind if I stroll around the cemetery and look at some other markers while we're here?" Allie asked.

Drake rifled his fingers through his hair and yawned. "Sure, why not? We're on vacation. Knock yourself out."

Allie thanked them and strolled off toward the tallest marker in the cemetery, a twenty-five-foot-tall obelisk.

"I thought they buried Benjamin Franklin in Philadelphia," Allie said, sensing someone beside her.

"He is buried in Philly," Ingrid said. "This marker is for his parents. I had a good time last night hanging out with you."

Allie looked over at Ingrid and smiled. "You know, I did too. Even though we did nothing but sit around and read and talk. It was nice. I don't have a lot of female friends with the same interests I have, so it's nice to spend time with someone who does."

Ingrid's cheeks turned a light pink from the complement. "Come on, let's find more dead people."

Ingrid interlocked arms with Allie and led her off to the next tall pillar they saw. When they got to the resting place of Paul Revere, Allie snapped a photo before they moved on to the large stone memorial for John Hancock.

"I like this one," Allie said as she stopped and pointed at the marker. The grave was above ground and looked large enough to contain a coffin. At the foot end was an intricate carving of what looked like a coat of arms. It included a family crest with a heart in the middle, and a knight's helmet with a bird standing on top of it.

Ingrid nodded. "Yeah, they don't make them like that anymore. The closest modern marker I've seen to this is a gravestone with granny's secret chocolate chip cookie recipe on the back."

"Whose grave is this?" Allie asked. "Peter Faneuil? I never heard of him."

"Oh, he was a rich guy who…" Ingrid trailed off and stared into Allie's eyes.

"Is there something on my face?" Allie asked.

Without responding, Ingrid took out her phone and looked up the history of Peter Faneuil, and then the building he gave to the city.

"What are you doing?" Allie asked.

Ingrid held up a finger to pause Allie, finished reading, then spoke. "Faneuil was this rich business guy who built Faneuil Hall, which was a market and a meeting place. After the British shot Crispus Attucks during the Boston Massacre, they took him to Faneuil Hall. He laid in state there until they buried him here, three days later."

"I'm not following you."

"Attucks rests. The message. Not his eternal rest here, but his temporary rest at Faneuil Hall."

Allie let out a squeak of excitement, then drew Ingrid in for a hug. "You're a genius! Let's go round up the lovebirds."

A half hour later, the quartet was standing before the tall statue of Samuel Adams. Despite Geneva's efforts, Drake continued to refer to him as 'the beer guy'. Beyond the statue stood the impressive three-story, red brick Faneuil Hall.

"Fancy," Drake said as he admired the architecture.

"Come on, there's a visitor's center inside. Let's go see what we can find out," Geneva said.

They stepped into the meeting hall and stopped just inside the entry and looked around. Like the name implied, the meeting hall had fifteen rows of wood chairs on either side of an aisle that ran from the entry door to the stage. Off in the wings was additional seating, and the second-floor balcony contained seats along the outside walls. A stage five feet high and faced with red, white, and blue bunting dominated the front of the room.

A wood lectern stood center stage in the front. Behind the lectern were several wood chairs to accommodate speakers. Behind the chairs along the back wall were marble busts of several Bostonians, including John Adams and Daniel Webster. Dominating the entire wall behind the stage was a massive painting of Daniel Webster debating Robert Hayne. Four other portraits hung on the walls, including one of Peter Faneuil himself.

Drake spotted a park ranger standing in the back corner of the room, looking bored. As Allie, Ingrid, and Geneva went off to explore the exhibits, Drake approached the ranger.

"Hello, quick question. Could you tell me if this is the original building from the 1700s?"

The young ranger shifted his stance and scratched his beard as he thought about it. "Well, there are elements of it that are original, but they redid most of the building over the years. It burned down in 1761, and they rebuilt it the next year. They expanded the building then, and added the third floor in 1806, and in 1898 they completely rebuilt it. They did the last major restoration in 1992. Does that answer your question?"

Drake's shoulders slumped in resignation, and he sighed. "Yes, thanks."

"You sound disappointed. Not get the answer you were looking for?"

Drake thought for a moment. "Not really. My redheaded friend over there is really interested in authentic artifacts from the American Revolution. We've come all the way from Nashville to see what we could see from that time period."

The ranger looked where Drake was pointing, which was at

Allie, who was busy snapping pictures of the artwork near the stage.

"Wait here, I'll be right back," the ranger said. He left the room and returned a couple minutes later, followed by another ranger.

"Steve here says I should give you and your friend the special tour," the new ranger said.

"Hold on, let me get my friend." Drake rush-walked across the room, grabbed Allie by the arm, and returned to the ranger.

"Allie, this is…"

"Folks called me Ranger Red for the longest time, because my hair is the color of yours." He ran his fingers through his white hair. "Of course, not so much anymore. Now I look like when the founding fathers wore those wigs, but twenty-five years ago, we'd have been mistaken for twins, you and I. Ready to go? Follow me."

Drake and Allie stepped behind the skinny ranger and followed him to the elevator. Once inside, he pushed the button for the fourth floor, and they waited patiently during the ride. The door opened, and Drake thought they were going to the Ancient and Honorable Artillery Company Museum that occupied the fourth floor. When they exited the elevator, Ranger Red took them down a corridor, then behind a door that was marked for employees only. Red flipped a light switch, and they found themselves in a large storage room. The building caretakers over time had stuffed the room with file cabinets, storage shelves, boxes, and crates of all shapes and sizes.

"This is where we hide the good stuff," Red explained. "Mostly items that people aren't interested in, or things we use for rotating displays. If you're looking for authentic artifacts that date back to the war, I've got two that may interest you. Follow me."

Red guided Drake and Allie over to the side of the room, where a large granite stone sat on a pallet. The engraving on the side read 1740.

"This was the original cornerstone when it was first built. The workers removed it in 1806 when the building underwent its first major renovation. Fortunately, someone had the foresight to save it."

"Can I touch it?" Allie asked.

Ranger Red grinned at her. "Go on ahead. It's survived three hundred years' worth of fires, construction, and wars, so I doubt you giving it a touch will cause it to crumble to dust at this point."

Allie smiled back, then crouched down to get a closer look at the stone. It looked pitted and well-worn, but she neither saw nor felt any indications of markings on it other than the date.

"What's the other item?" Allie said as she got back to her feet.

"The crown jewel, and my absolute favorite." Red waved them along and picked their way through a tight aisle of metal shelves.

"Wait," Drake said as he stopped and pointed at a box. "Are these really Paul Revere's shoes?"

Red backtracked, picked the plastic storage box from the shelf, opened it up, and held it so everyone could see inside. The box contained a pair of black leather shoes with a rectangular silver belt on the front. "Looks like it to me," Red said. He closed the box, returned it to the shelf, and continued on.

In the far corner of the room, set into a concrete block, was a four-foot-high weathervane with a giant grasshopper on top, gilded in gold leaf.

"What do you think?" Red said. "Impressive, isn't it?"

"Isn't this the same as the one on top of the building?" Allie asked.

Red leaned in closer, and whispered, as if there was someone else around who could hear them. "I'll let you in on a secret. This one's the original, made in 1742. After thieves returned it in 1974, we put up a reproduction instead. Go ahead. Look at it. It's an amazing work of art."

"Can I touch this?" Allie asked.

Red laughed a hearty laugh. "Lightning has struck it several times. I'm sure it can handle you!"

Allie leaned in and examined the vane closely. Something caught her attention, so she looked back at Drake and gave him a nod.

Drake caught the meaning, turned around, and pointed back into the heart of the room. "Hey, Ranger Red, besides Revere's shoes, what other treasures did you hide away up here?"

Drake and Red stepped away from the weathervane and disappeared among the shelves. Once they were gone, Allie quickly retrieved her phone and snapped off a few pictures. She reviewed them, and, satisfied with what she had, rejoined the others where she found Ranger Red showing Drake a small box of uniform buttons.

"Hey, Drake, we should get a move on. Geneva and Ingrid are probably wondering where we are. Red, thank you. This has been wonderful."

Rather than wait for the elevator, Allie and Drake rushed down the stairs, and found Geneva and Ingrid sitting on chairs inside the hall.

"Where have you been?" Geneva asked.

"Let's go outside," Allie said. "I could really use some sun."

CHAPTER TEN

Allie led the group outside, and they found an empty park bench near the statue of Samuel Adams to sit on.

"Where did you guys disappear to?" Geneva asked.

"Got a special tour to check out Paul Revere's shoes. They were pretty fancy," Drake answered.

Geneva stared at Drake with an expression of disbelief on her face.

Drake reached over, took her hand in hers. "It's true. I asked the ranger in there if they had any artifacts from back in the day, and he got one of the other rangers who gave Allie and me a backstage tour of the place. They have like a billion pieces of history tucked away behind a door on the top floor."

"Including one that had these on it," Allie said. She passed her phone around and showed everyone the small, hand-etched letters, looking like graffiti in the golden gilding.

"Where did you find this?" Ingrid asked.

"On the original weathervane. The one that's up there now is a replica."

Ingrid looked back at the pictures and thought about the letters scratched into the grasshopper: SVRUQ MCGIL VCFMS FDWIW QRTPW GJKG. "Another cipher?"

Allie nodded. "For sure. Not Caesar, though. This one's a little harder."

"Let me see if can run it through a few code breakers and see what we come up with," Ingrid said.

Ingrid dug out her phone, transcribed the letters into the notepad, and handed Allie's phone back to her. She brought up her favorite puzzle solving app and copied the letter string from the clipboard to the app and started the decryption. She looked up and caught her friends watching her.

"You know, this would go faster if everyone helped," Ingrid said.

"Yeah, probably," Drake admitted. "What's the letters?"

Allie brought up the picture again and held out her phone for Geneva and Drake to see. Withing a minute, all four of them were trying out different ciphers and ideas for solutions. As they failed, they called out the ones that didn't work, and after thirty minutes, they gave up.

Allie set her phone down and leaned back on the bench. She stretched her arms above her head, interlaced her fingers, and tried to touch the sky. She twisted her torso to the left, to the right, and finally released her hands and let them fall to her sides.

"Maybe we should give this up. Do something else, like visit other touristy things, or perhaps find some more geocaches," Allie said. "I mean, it's not like any of us are actually expecting to find a king's ransom worth of buried treasure that is still out there after three hundred years."

Drake shook his head. "Tsk, tsk, Allie. Where's your sense of adventure?"

Allie picked up her phone and opened her geocaching app

to see if there were any geocaches nearby. "Hey, there's a virtual cache only point one-one from here. I'm going to go for it. Anyone want to come?"

"Is it the Boston Massacre site one?" Geneva asked.

Allie checked the app. "Yep. You already have that one?"

"Yes. I'll keep trying to crack the code. I'll wait for you here."

"I'll stay here, too," Drake said. "I'm sure I can figure this out."

Allie rolled her eyes and shook her head. Drake was good for some puzzles, but he hated things like ciphers with a passion and usually relied on her to crack the code and get the answers.

"I'll go with you," Ingrid said as she got to her feet. "My back is getting stiff from too much sitting. Let's go."

Allie went to check the compass for the directions to the geocache, but Ingrid stopped her.

"There's no need for that. I've been there before," she said.

After they were out of earshot of the others, Ingrid whispered to Allie. "You know, he wasn't even trying to solve that cipher. I noticed him looking at sports scores on his phone instead."

Allie laughed. "I don't know. Maybe he's on to something. Perhaps the founding fathers were so smart, they included a message about the Red Sox - Yankees game and they hid the next clue by the left field foul pole at Fenway."

Ingrid smiled. "I'm sure that's the line he's taking. He's not so good with the puzzles?"

"You could say that. He's my good friend, and I love him to death, but he's honestly not that great at them. He doesn't mind the simple things, like finding coordinates in word searches, or Sudoku grids. And he's pretty good at the ones where you only need to look up answers on the Internet, but when you get into cipher territory, he tunes out. It's simply not in his wheelhouse."

"Are there any geocaches that aren't your thing?" Ingrid asked.

"Of course. I don't like it when EarthCaches are overly complicated. I mean, I know you're supposed to learn something from them, but I don't like it when the cache owner gets carried away. Estimate the height or width of a waterfall? I can do that. Determine the flow rate of a natural spring? I can do that, too. I visited one in Tennessee where I had to count the fossils in a wall, which I was good with. But man, when you get questions about having to determine the specific type of rock in an area. And come up with the exact measurement and a scientific theory of how the rock formed over a billion years? Nope, that's when I draw the line. If I read the description and I think it's something that I'd only be able to answer with a doctorate in geology, I skip it."

Ingrid nodded. "Believe me, I know what you mean. I'm not a fan of geocaches placed on a ledge, or on a high bridge. I'm always afraid I'm going to fall, even if my rational mind tells me I'm perfectly safe."

"Oh, and I dislike caches that are in caves, or underground. I mean, I'll do them, especially if I can still sense sunlight, but I try to avoid those," Allie admitted.

"That we can agree on. I don't like them either," Ingrid said. "We're almost there. Notice that ring over there in the concrete? That's the site."

They stopped at the outer edge of the marker, and Allie reopened her app to check the qualifications for the find. "Upload a picture of you or your GPS at the site of the Boston Massacre and answer the question of what animals are watching you. Do not post the answer in your log or I will delete it. Seems easy enough."

Allie turned in a circle and checked if any animals were around. Other than a woman walking a Pekingese with golden fur, she didn't observe any non-humans. She spun around a second time, still saw nothing, but she heard Ingrid giggle.

"Are you enjoying watching me make a fool of myself?"

Ingrid giggled again. "Of course. You look so cute when you do it."

"Okay smarty-pants. What's the answer?"

Ingrid stepped behind Allie, grabbed her shoulders, and turned her until she faced a red brick building. Then she lifted Allie's right arm and pointed it at the roof. "How's that for a hint?"

Allie looked up, and above her there were two statues, one on each corner of the roof. "A lion and a horse?"

"It's not a horse. It's a unicorn," Ingrid corrected.

Allie squinted, and saw that indeed, a long horn extended from the horse's forehead. "Okay. It's a unicorn." Allie typed the answers into the app and sent them off. "Picture time. Get in here with me."

Allie turned so her back was to the marker and held the phone high so she could get a selfie with it. Ingrid moved into the shot.

"You need to get closer. I only have half of your face in frame," Allie said.

Ingrid moved in closer still, and a moment later, Allie could feel the heat coming from the soft flesh of Ingrid's cheek.

"Perfect," Allie said. "Now smile."

They did, and after Allie snapped the photo, Ingrid pulled away. "Let's get one more."

Ingrid moved in close again, and a second before Allie pushed the button, Ingrid turned her head and kissed Allie lightly on the cheek. Allie snapped the shot, and Ingrid pulled back away, embarrassed.

Allie, unflinching, brought up the photo and showed it to Ingrid. "Looks good. You take a splendid picture."

Ingrid smiled. "It's in the Danish genes I have."

Allie reached out and grabbed Ingrid's hand. "Let's go back. If we leave those two alone, who knows what trouble they'll get into?"

Without speaking, the two walked back to Faneuil Hall and took their original seats on the bench.

"You find what you were looking for?" Drake asked without looking up from his phone.

"Oh, yes I did," Allie answered. "How's the code breaking going?"

Geneva shook her head. "Not so good. I've hit a brick wall every time I've tried something."

"Did you try a Vigenère cipher?" Ingrid asked.

"No," Geneva said. "Those are impossible to crack without a keyword."

From where they were sitting, Allie could barely see a large golden insect that appeared to be standing on the roof of the building. "Try grasshopper."

Geneva shrugged, then put the word grasshopper in as the keyword. "Well, I'll be a monkey's aunt. You got it. Mercy for the woman with many words."

"Mercy for the woman with many words? What does that mean?" Drake asked. "What woman needs mercy? For what words? All we've done is uncover another riddle."

"True, but at least this one's in English. I'll go ask Red and see if he can shed any light on it," Allie said.

"Did she find her cache?" Drake asked Ingrid as they watched Allie walk toward the building's entrance.

"Oh yeah," Ingrid said.

"Did she have any trouble with the animals?" Geneva asked.

"She only spun in a circle twice before I helped her out."

Ingrid and Geneva laughed, knowing what they'd gone through.

"What's so funny?" Drake asked.

"You should have seen us when we did that cache. We must have looked in every window within viewing distance of that site before Ingrid had the common sense enough to just look up," Geneva said.

"And that was an accident. I was following a helicopter that was flying over us," Ingrid admitted. "She's coming back fast. Must not have gotten what we need."

The three peered at Allie as she walked toward them, then she stopped without sitting back down. "Red is incredible. I think he knows everything about the American Revolution."

Drake snickered. "He's old enough to have probably lived through it."

Allie ignored the comment. "It turns out we were on the wrong track. It's not to give mercy to a woman with many words. There was a woman back then named Mercy who used a lot of words. She was a big-time revolutionary who was heavily into politics, and was also a writer who published several articles, poems, and plays. Mercy Warren was her name."

"I don't suppose Red had her complete bibliography tucked away in a dusty box up there, did he?" Drake asked.

"No. But he suggested we go visit a library nearby. Apparently, they digitized a lot of her writings, and they are available with the touch of a button. Let's get going. It's only a few blocks from here."

After a five-block hike, they stepped into the local library, and had a brief chat with the head librarian, who directed them to the local history section. It wasn't a large room, considering the sheer amount of local history that Boston and the surrounding region had accumulated over the roughly four hundred years of Boston's existence. But there was enough space for three walls worth of shelves. The shelves held everything from city directories, to handwritten journals, to volumes of homemade family genealogies, and ship's passenger manifests. The room held anything related to local history that didn't fit in nicely on the neat stack in the main library.

Also in the room were four small cubicles, two of which held desktop computers, and two which held microfilm machines. A quick round robin of rock-paper-scissors determined that Drake and Ingrid would search through the digital records. Geneva, in third place, got to handle the microfiche. Allie, the first one out of the game, got the arduous task of checking the physical stacks to see if there was anything to find on the mysterious Mercy Warren.

Ingrid was more computer-savvy than Drake and quickly found a treasure trove of information. "Hey, I've got lots of hits here," she said as she leaned back in her chair and pointed at the screen. "You said she was a writer, Allie, but I didn't expect her to be this prolific. There are references to several plays, as well as a bunch of poems, and a few books as well. I don't even know where to start."

Drake leaned over and looked at Ingrid's screen and the list of search results it contained. "Can you sort that by date?"

Ingrid poked at the keys and, after a few seconds, got the list in ascending order by publication date, then moved aside so Drake could get a closer look.

"I'd say based on the other clues we've followed, you should probably concentrate on anything published before, let's say, 1776. What do you get then?"

"I've got four plays for sure. Some poetry had early dates. And there was a book published of some of her personal letters to some of the heavy hitters of the day, including Washington and Jefferson."

Drake nodded. "Hold on." Drake got up and walked over to a small table just inside the entrance of the room and selected from it a sheet of paper and a pencil. He rejoined Ingrid and copied down the file names of the first three items on the list, then sat at his own computer. "You start from line four on down. Whoever finishes first helps the other."

Ingrid nodded, clicked on the first file, and began to scan through the play *The Adulateur*.

"How are you doing, Allie?" Drake asked.

Allie was busy at one shelf of books, running her fingers from spine to spine as she read the titles. "Fine. Have found nothing remotely related to her yet. I found a copy of an old family cookbook, so if you need a good recipe for corn porridge, or instructions on how to make your own cheese, I've got you covered."

Drake laughed and turned his attention to Geneva, who was getting irritated with a microfilm reader that wasn't working correctly. Every time she fed the spool of film through the machine and tried to advance it with the control knob, the end would slip. Then it would feed back out and spin around until it dropped off the spool. Watching her fight with the machine was like viewing an old Charlie Chaplin movie.

"Hey, Geneva?" Drake said.

Geneva turned and gave Drake the death stare she'd been using on the machine for the past few minutes.

"Um, never mind," he said as he turned his attention back to his computer.

Geneva turned her attention back to the microfilm and removed the spool from the spindle. She carefully rewound the spool to get the film back on, then pulled it taut so it wouldn't spill off again. Keeping it taut, she took her time feeding the film between two rollers, between the glass plates, then through two rollers on the other side. For the last step, she tucked the film end into the slot, applied tension on the receiving wheel, then spun it with her fingers until the reel took up film. She crossed her fingers, then turned the fast-forward knob just a touch. The film finally cooperated, and the front page of the *Boston Gazette* appeared on the screen.

Geneva had her own notepad, and she checked the list of five entries for the first date, then compared the date on the paper's masthead to that on her list. She fast-forwarded through two years' worth of weekly newspapers before she slowed the machine and eventually got to the issue she wanted. There, on the first page, was a poem that argued for independence over twenty-seven lines. Although it was stirring, there was nothing about it that looked peculiar. Geneva moved on to the second one, published only three months later, and that poem took an unkind view of George III. The third poem spoke of the evils of taxation without representation, and the fourth, published in the first week of December 1776, was an ode to an old church. Next to the entry, she jotted down the microfiche page number, then moved forward until she got to the fifth and final poem. The last poem turned out to be a rousing call for the citizens to take up arms against injustice.

"Hey, guys, I think I found something odd," Geneva said.

Allie sat down in the unoccupied chair, and Drake and Ingrid shifted their seats so they could see better.

Geneva fed the fiche backward until she found the page number for the fourth poem. "I looked up five poems in the

Boston Gazette that were attributed to Mercy Warren. Four out of the five were all rallying cries to spur the locals into war with Britain, but she titled the fourth *The Crypt 'Neath the Church."*

"Can you make that bigger?" Drake asked.

Geneva adjusted a couple of knobs, and the text became larger on the screen. Silently, and at their own pace, the four read the poem.

"You're right, this poem seems out of place," Drake admitted. "Why would a newspaper print this, especially with a war right around the corner? What church is this referring to even? It's a little vague, isn't it?"

"Not really. Based on the year, I'd say it's Christ Church," Ingrid said.

"Is there a chance it's still standing?" Allie asked.

Geneva grinned. "You bet your boots it's still standing. It's one of the oldest churches in America, although now it's commonly known as the Old North Church. You know, of one if by land, two if by sea fame."

CHAPTER ELEVEN

A half an hour later, they were in line, waiting to gain entry into the old church. Slowly, they traveled the cobblestone sidewalk between the church and the gift shop, and they waited patiently until it was their turn to enter.

Drake waited in line behind an old couple wearing American flag shirts. When they shifted, he spotted a brochure on the counter that attracted his attention, so he reached out around the man and took one. He only had a few seconds to scan the brochure before the person behind the counter called him forward to pay the entrance fee.

"Can we do the crypt tour?"

"How many?" the teenage ticket seller asked.

"Four."

She clicked a couple of buttons on the computer. "There's room for four on the tour that starts in a half hour. Does that work for you?"

"Sure does," Drake said as he dug his credit card from his wallet and passed it to her.

The transaction completed, she handed him back his card, along with four tickets. "Inside you'll see a sign where the tour starts. I recommend you get there five minutes early because the tour starts right on the hour. No refunds."

"Thanks," Drake said. He turned and passed a ticket out to everyone in his group. "We've got twenty minutes to kill before we enter the crypt, so we can go in and look around in the meantime."

They stepped into the church proper and looked around. White was the dominant color inside the church. The entire floor contained box pews, which resembled modern day office cubicles. Only three aisles running from the back to the front of the room broke up the space.

Each box pew had waist-high walls, painted white with wood trim on the tops. And each had a small door that swung out, and every door contained a brass plaque. The plaques listed the pew number, along with the name of the parishioner who owned them, and the year they owned it. Inside the box were white-painted wood pews, along with modern hymnals for worshippers to use during modern Sunday services.

The front of the church held the altar and an elevated pulpit. In the back were stairs that led to the upper gallery, which contained additional pews, as well as an impressive-looking organ.

Along the walls between the open windows were various historical displays, and memorials dedicated to past members. Allie, being Allie, made a tour around the room, reading every available sign.

Drake checked the time, saw he still had twenty minutes to wait until the crypt tour, opened a door to a box, and sat down on the pew. Geneva slid into the spot next to him, and he reached for her hand.

"Fancy church, huh?" Drake said. "Can you picture them throwing a lantern up in the belfry and starting Revere's ride?"

"No, not really," Geneva admitted.

Drake chuckled. "Yeah, me neither. I'll bet Allie can, though. Visualizing herself in historical contexts is like her superpower."

"That's not necessarily a bad thing," Geneva said.

"Oh, no, I didn't say it was. It only becomes a problem when we're on a time schedule. Actually, I've been quite proud of her for the past couple of days. She seems focused, and isn't wandering off to check out every statue, plaque, and historical marker she sees."

Geneva let go of Drake's hand and scratched the back of his neck gently. "It seems we have been rushing through this town. Doesn't seem like the laid-back vacation experience I had in my head."

Drake nodded. "Yeah, same here. I think I've gotten a little nutty with the treasure thing. Perhaps it's best if we pull back the throttle on that and get back to finding geocaches and seeing the sights."

"And don't forget about going to the symphony."

Drake grinned. "There's no way I would forget about that! It's what I'm looking forward to the most!"

"What's that?" Ingrid asked as she entered the box and took the seat next to Geneva. Allie, who also appeared from nowhere, stood outside the box and leaned over the wall.

"Heading to the symphony on Friday night," Drake answered. "Aren't you looking forward to it?"

"For sure I am," Ingrid gushed. "I wouldn't miss it for the entire world."

Geneva laughed. "You're such a liar."

Ingrid put a mock look of taken offense on her face. "Who?

Me?"

"Yes, you. You hate classical music. The only time you like to hear violins is when they're used as fiddles in country music," Geneva teased.

"Ooh, you'd fit right in Nashville," Allie said with a smile. "Come to town and I'll take you around to all the country bars."

"I enjoyed the symphony concert you took me to a couple of years ago," Ingrid said.

"You mean when we went to see the Fourth of July show?" Geneva asked.

Ingrid nodded. "Yes, that was the one."

"First off, that was the Boston Pops, not the Boston Symphony. And, as I recall, you liked the fireworks show more than any of the music they played that night."

Ingrid shrugged. "Okay, so I like the fireworks. So, sue me."

"Hey," Drake interrupted, "Geneva and I were just talking about this treasure thing, and we both agree that I've gotten out of control trying to pursue it. I mean, it's probably been gone for forever, if it even really existed at all. I think we should slow down and get back to geocaching and being tourists. What do you say?"

Allie looked at Ingrid, then at Geneva.

"Don't all speak at once," Drake said. "It's hard to hear you over the others. Ingrid, what do you think?"

Ingrid pointed at Allie. "Ask her. She's a guest here."

Allie felt the weight of three sets of eyes staring at her. She gathered her thoughts, then exhaled slowly. "Actually, I don't think the treasure hunting thing has been too bad. I mean, so far, it's taken us to these historical places I wanted to visit while we were here. Like right now, I mean, we're already here, and we already have tickets for the tour, so why would we not hunt for clues while we're down there?"

"So, to clarify, we're still on the hunt?" Drake asked.

Allie thought for a moment. "Okay, new rules. One, we slow down the pace. We don't have to rush around like mad. Let's take it easy, stop for lunch, enjoy the nice day. And we find caches, and we see more things of interest. And if any of us decides it's too much, we give it up."

Drake nodded. "That's reasonable. Okay with y'all?"

Geneva and Ingrid nodded.

"Good," Drake said. "New plan. We'll finish with the crypt tour, then find something else to do besides chase a mystery all over town." Drake looked at his watch. "Speaking of the tour, it's about time we head over there."

Allie walked up the aisle to give the others enough room to leave the box, and they made their way to the sign pointing the way to the crypt tour. Five minutes before the tour was about to depart, a guide appeared and starting checking tickets. It was a light tour. Besides the four friends, the only other couple interested in the macabre adventure was the couple who had entered the museum just before them.

"Can I have your attention, please? My name is John and I'll be your guide down into the crypts. Just a few comments before we go. The stairs and the floor are uneven in spots, so please watch your footing. And there are areas down there that can be tight, so if you're claustrophobic, I recommend you stay up here. In places it's also dimly lit, so please be cautious. There's no eating or drinking on the tour, and out of respect for those interred below, please don't touch. Anyone have questions before we go?"

Allie raised her hand. "Can we take pictures, John?"

"Photographs are fine, but please, no selfie sticks because of the tight quarters," John answered.

"Are selfie sticks still a thing?" Ingrid whispered to Allie.

Allie shrugged. "I have no clue."

"Please, now follow me, be careful, and stick together," John ordered.

The group followed John through a corridor, and that corridor led to a flight of stone stairs. As they descended, their footsteps echoed against the stone walls, and the temperature decreased. When they finally arrived at the bottom, John stepped a few feet into the main corridor to give everyone room to enter.

"Please remember to watch your footing," John advised, as he waited for people to cluster around him.

Drake was the last one down the stairs. When he got to the bottom, he joined the group and looked around. The floor was a gray concrete that reminded him of his garage floor at home. The walls were brick, but not a consistent color. They ranged from a deep maroon to red, to brown, to white, and there was a light film of dust that covered everything and swirled around people's feet as they stepped. Above the corridor, a line of single-bulb lights strung along at several-foot intervals provided the only light.

"Just a little background," John said. "Here beneath the church, there are thirty-seven brick vaults and each one can hold twenty to forty coffins. Burials down here started in 1732 and ended in 1860."

"How many people did they bury down here?" the woman asked.

"Around eleven hundred is the best guess, although there could be more," John answered. "Please, step this way."

"And they don't bury people down here anymore?" the woman asked.

John stopped in his tracks. "No. The city of Boston ordered that all burials in crypts stop, and all the vaults sealed in 1853. It ended because of ongoing health concerns for the general population. But the church didn't halt burials until 1860, when the courts stepped in and compelled every cemetery and church to comply with the new law."

"It must not have smelled very good with the bodies down here," the lady said.

A sly smile crossed John's face. "No. It must not have. In fact, there are air vents that lead from the crypt to below the windows upstairs to allow for air circulation down here. It doesn't take much of an imagination to guess what it was like to be at church in the heat of the summer. Come, follow me."

The group shuffled along behind John, stopped when he did, and formed a semi-circle around the tomb he was standing before.

"Before you is the tomb of Major John Pitcairn, who got shot six times during the Battle of Bunker Hill, including once in the head. His son ferried him across the river, and he later died of his wounds."

"Why would they bury him here and not send him back to England?" Geneva asked.

"Back then, this was an Anglican church, connected to the Church of England, so it wasn't unusual for British subjects to be buried in one. In fact, they interred several other British officers here with Pitcairn. If you'll notice, right next door is the tomb of Samuel Weekes. His wife, Elizabeth, died in 1721 while at sea on the way to America, leaving Samuel without a wife or any children. So, when he bought this tomb, he shared it with his friends, as seen in the old inscription there. Note the differences between the two markers. The Weekes marker is most likely to be original to the era, while the one for Major Pitcairn was most likely placed here in the early to mid-1800s."

John waited for the group to take photographs, then moved down the corridor.

Since he was at the back of the pack, Drake waited until the group left, then turned and rushed along the short corridor behind him. He scanned each tomb door, looking for any clues that had anything to do with the poem by Mercy Warren. He rushed his way through, not wanting to take too much time away from the group. Because of the tight quarters and the fact that they sealed each tomb closed, he felt confident that he didn't miss a thing. Just in case, he snapped photographs of every piece of writing he came across. Drake rushed his way back to the group and slowed as he caught up to them. He tried to pretend that he'd been with them the entire time, and he returned to find John in mid-lecture.

"So, if you'll compare this tomb door to some others we've seen, you can see that this one, leading to the tomb of Shubael Bell, is clearly made of iron. Stone, iron, and wood were the three options for creating tomb doors down here, and no one is clear why there were different materials for the different doors. Sir, did you find what you were looking for?"
Everyone turned and looked at Drake, since he was the only other sir in the group.

"Yeah. Sorry. I was just taking pictures of the different tombs. History nut. Sorry."

"Okay, fine. If you want to take photos, please do so, and if I'm going too fast for you, I'm happy to slow down, but please keep up with the group," John said.

"Okay. Sorry again," Drake said.

John nodded, then guided the group farther down the corridor.

Allie waited for Drake to catch up to her, then elbowed him in the ribs. "You got busted!" she whispered.

Drake snickered. "Yeah, I did. Come on. We need to get moving. I don't want to get sent to the principal's office."

Drake stopped long enough to snap a picture of the tombs

as they walked past, but he was never over five feet behind the tour.

"Here's an interesting one. Number fourteen, the stranger's tomb, from 1813. Who's behind the door? Who knows? Some say it's one of the many ghosts that inhabit the crypt," John said.

John turned and went on with the tour, and Drake waited until everyone had cleared the area before he stepped in and snapped a photo of the crypt.

"Well? What do you think?" Allie asked.

"I think we're probably at a dead end here. I mean, for all we know, they sealed the next clue inside a tomb. John was unhappy with me leaving the tour for three minutes. I can't imagine it would thrill him if I started breaking down walls and disturbing the dead."

"Probably not. There would be ghosts haunting you forever then," Allie agreed.

"I can't have that. I can barely put up with you haunting me every day," Drake teased.

"You're such a turd!"

"I know. Come on, we're falling behind."

Drake and Allie rushed to catch up with the group, but Drake still stopped several times to click photos of various tombs along the way. When they rejoined the others, they got there just in time to see the American flag wearing woman pointing to a small iron door. It was two-feet square, near the bottom of the floor.

"What's that?" The woman asked.

"Good eye. Of all the tombs in the place, that is the one that garners the most questions. Open the door," John said.

"Wait, what? We're not supposed to touch anything."

"This is the one exception to the rule. Go ahead."

The woman bent at the waist and opened the door. The

small iron door opened freely, although not without a squeak reminiscent of every haunted house movie ever produced. Everyone bent over to look at what was behind the door, but it was dark and hard to see. John pulled a flashlight from a belt clip and illuminated the area.

Behind the door was a small tomb marker, just a shade smaller than the door that hid it. Carved into the center of a marker were five concentric circles. The inner circle was about the size of a quarter, the others radiated out every inch. At the center of the inner circle, six shapes resembling flower petals reached out with their outer tips that ended at the outer circle. Above the crude etching were the initials 'O.D.E.', and beneath the etching were the words 'G.C., Witch Man'.

"What the heck is that?" Geneva asked.

"According to our researchers, that is an apotropaic mark, also known as a witch mark. It's a pattern used to protect from witchcraft," John explained.

"You're saying there's a witch buried in there? Why would someone bury a witch in a church? And why is that door so little?" Ingrid asked.

"No one knows for sure. Experts have x-rayed the wall, and there is indeed something in there that looks like it could be a small urn, but we've never opened or disturbed it."

"Why not?" Ingrid asked.

"There's never been a reason to. We opened many of the tombs when we upgraded the church with power, water, and fire suppression systems, but because this one wasn't in the way, we didn't touch it. This is still a crypt, so we don't like to disturb the remains unless it's absolutely necessary. Besides, folklore has it that if you disturb the grave of a witch, the witch will rise again."

John leaned forward, shut the door, and turned off his flashlight. "And with that, we've come to the end of the tour. Are there questions I can answer for anyone?"

No one said anything, so John pointed to the exit. "Good. I hope you enjoyed yourselves down here, and I hope you learned something. Watch yourselves on the stairs up, and I hope you all have a great rest of the day."

The stairs were behind them, so Drake was first in line to climb up to the street level. Without speaking, he left the church. In the church's courtyard, he sat down on a stone bench and waited for the others to join him.

"What's going on, Drake?" Geneva asked, the first to reach him.

Drake took out his phone, opened it to the last picture he took, and enlarged the photo. "Who can tell me something about witches?"

CHAPTER TWELVE

"Sure. I'll bet if we took a trip up to Salem, we would learn all we wanted to know about witches. But not today," Geneva said.

"No, I didn't mean today," Drake said. "What I meant was—"

Drake stopped speaking when Ingrid raised her hand to cut him off.

"Can we walk? I'd like to leave," Ingrid said.

Without a word, Drake stood, the others followed suit, and they trudged out of the courtyard.

"Where to? Should we return to the hotel?"

Ingrid looked around her as she hesitated. "Sure."

They strolled along Salem Street, following the narrow sidewalk, Drake and Geneva in front, Ingrid and Allie a few steps behind. They set a leisurely pace, not in a hurry to get anywhere, which allowed them to more appreciate the eclectic mix of shops as they wandered.

Ingrid stopped at a bakery and looked in the window.

"Those cakes look good, don't they?" Ingrid said as she

pointed to a three-tiered wedding cake with pearls piped in around the base of each layer. "Do you like cake, Allie?"

Allie joined Ingrid at the window and peered in. "Of course. As long as it has buttercream frosting. I'm a snob that way."

"I agree. If it doesn't have buttercream, I'd rather not have it."

Ingrid made a show by pointing to something else in the window. "I think your boyfriend is following us."

Allie tilted her head in confusion. "I'm not sure what you mean."

"The book guy," Ingrid clarified.

"Stan? The one who showed up at the restaurant yesterday?"

"Yep."

"Are you sure it was him?"

"Pretty sure. He was peeking around the corner when we were sitting in the courtyard. I only spotted him for a second and he stopped. I didn't know if I should mention it or not."

Allie gave a quick glance in the direction from which they came. She didn't recognize anyone who looked familiar among the many pedestrians traveling in either direction on both sides of the street.

"Can you tie my shoes for me? My knee hurts and I don't want to bend down," Allie asked.

Ingrid looked down at Allie's shoes. She had both perfectly tied, double knotted, with each loop the same size as the others. "Your shoes are fine."

"Please, don't argue, just do it." Allie turned her body, so she was facing down the street, and Ingrid crouched and pretended to retie Allie's shoes. As Ingrid pulled at the loops, Allie studied the street. Most people were walking with a purpose. She spotted a two-man crew washing the windows of a bank a half of a block away, and a steady stream of people going in and out of a delicatessen. She counted three people in suits chatting on cell phones as they rushed to their destinations. Down the street walked a small group of tourists being led by a guide using an old car antenna with a red ribbon tied to the top as a flag. The tourists were coming toward Allie. She thought the group of eleven were going to squeeze past them on the sidewalk, but at the last second, they took a left and walked across the intersection. As the last of the group cleared Allie's sight line, she spotted Stan, trying to look like a tourist interested in whatever window he was peering into.

"I got him. He's about a block back from us," Allie said. "You can stand up now."

Ingrid stood and brushed off the knees of her pants, even though they hadn't touched the concrete. "What should we do?" Ingrid asked.

"I guess carry on with our day. Maybe it's a coincidence that he's here."

"A coincidence? I'm sure it is. And during the winter, I play quarterback for the New England Bills," Ingrid said.

Allie grinned. "Patriots. Buffalo is the Bills."

"Whatever. You understood what I meant."

"Yes, I get your drift. Come on, let's catch up to the others."

Allie and Ingrid walked quickly until they caught back up with Drake and Geneva two blocks later, and once there, Allie told the others they had a tail.

"Okay, so what are we going to do about it?" Geneva asked.

"I think we should confront him," Drake answered without hesitation. "It's obvious to me he's stalking Allie, and we should put an end to it right now, before this goes any further."

Allie placed a hand on Drake's chest to stop his rant. "Hold on there, big fella. How can you be sure it's all about me?"

"Um, because I've got eyes, and I noticed the way he leered at you at the restaurant yesterday. He was practically drooling over you."

"I'm still not convinced it's all about me," Allie said. "Look, there's a crowded bookstore up ahead. Let's keep walking, and when we pass it, I'll dip in there and hide and you three keep going. Then we can see if he comes after me for sure, or if it's all of us he's interested in."

"Or it might be a coincidence," Ingrid said.

"Right, or he simply ends up going his own way."

"What happens if he follows you, and we're not there to protect you?" Drake asked.

"Simple. I go up to the counter and ask someone to call the cops. It's a crowded building. Even if he was the stalker supreme, I doubt that he'd pull something with dozens of witnesses around."

Drake thought about it and nodded. "Okay. I'm not stoked about the idea, but let's see what happens."

The group started walking again, and Allie stepped a little faster to take the lead position. When they passed the large bookstore, Allie slipped into the door, and the other three kept strolling right on by without so much as a pause.

The bookstore had a large picture window at the front of the building. In full view of that window were two large wooden tables on which were displays of new arrivals, and a sign that announced an upcoming author signing event. Beyond the table display were shelves that came to two inches below Allie's shoulder height, so Allie placed herself behind the bookcase. She picked a random book from the shelf and propped it open and stood it up on end to use it as cover. Allie checked her position and determined she had not only a good view of the window and saw everyone that passed by, but she also had a view of the door. She examined anyone who entered, and all the while, she was confident that no one could see her. Just in case, she surveyed her surroundings and plotted out the best route to reach the checkout counter if anything wrong happened.

Allie waited. She ignored anyone outside walking from her right to her left and concentrated on those coming from the other way. The door opened, and Allie watched as a grandmother with a young girl in tow stepped into the store. Less than a minute later, a teenage boy wearing a basketball jersey and carrying a skateboard entered.

Allie counted off the seconds in her head, and she got all the way to ninety-three when Stan walked past the window without stopping. Allie did a ten count and was about to leave her hiding space, when suddenly, Stan reappeared and walked to the center of the window. He held his hand over his eyes to ease the glare as he looked into the store. He scanned from left to right and reversed direction, and a heartbeat later, he was gone again.

Allie didn't realize she had been holding her breath, but based on the burning in her lungs, she knew she was for at least forty seconds. She waited another few moments for Stan to return, and when he didn't, Allie made for the front door.

She wanted to play it coy, open the door, stick her head out, and make sure the coast was clear. A large man with two bags bulging with books foiled that plan when he practically pushed Allie out into the street as he exited. Allie panicked, knowing she'd blown her cover, but when she looked up the street, she saw Stan nowhere in sight.

Allie walked to the end of the block, stopped and peeked around the corner to discover if Stan was there, but he wasn't. She continued on, knowing the route Drake and the others were planning to take to the hotel, and increased her rate of speed. She knew the others had planned to dally, so she guessed she'd encounter them sooner than later.

The buildings fell away when she left the claustrophobic feeling of Salem Street and stepped across the road onto the Rose Kennedy Greenway. Her knee ached, and she spotted a table where there were two men playing chess. She thought about asking to sit down at one of the two spare chairs near them when a woman with a stroller vacated a park bench only a few feet away.

Allie sat on the bench and swung sideways so she could put her leg up on the seat and rubbed her sore knee. She considered for a moment calling for an Uber, but being the stubborn soul she was, resolved to keep going. Allie knew all she needed to do was get back to her room, and the rest of the night would be one with little tromping around the city.

As she rested, Allie took her backpack from her shoulders, fished out a bottle of water, and had a drink. She checked through all the various pockets for the small bottle of ibuprofen she usually carried but couldn't find it. Allie closed her eyes, thought for a moment, and remembered it was sitting on the sink in the hotel bathroom where she'd last taken some pills. She took another drink, swished the water around in her mouth to knock back some of the dryness, swallowed, and returned the bottle to her pack.

She looked across the park and, wanting not to push it too much, eyed her next potential spot to sit. It was where the brick path dipped to become flush with the next street over. Next to the path was a wall that she estimated would be hip height, a perfect spot to rest once she got across the park. Allie swung her leg over and got to her feet. She took three steps and stood stone still when she spotted Stan.

Allie had been so focused on the wall; she hadn't noticed the large bush that separated the park from the street. Just at the edge of that bush, she spotted Stan standing there. To her surprise, he didn't focus on her. Rather, he paid close attention to something ahead of them. She watched him for a while, and not once did he glance behind him.

She opened her backpack again and fished out a light blue windbreaker and a Tennessee Titans baseball cap. She put them on, added her sunglasses to complete her disguise, and ambled toward the other end of the park. Allie made it halfway through the space when Stan looked both ways, then crossed the street against the light.

Although her knee was throbbing, Allie picked up the pace and rushed to the corner. The light turned green, and the little man on the walk signal said to go, so Allie stepped out into the street. Before she could take a second step, someone grabbed her by the shoulder and pulled her back onto the sidewalk. She was about to turn around and confront the stranger, but before she could, a taxi blew the light and sped through the crosswalk.

Her anger dissipated, and Allie turned around and saw a woman in shorts and a sports bra running in place.

"Thanks," Allie said.

"No problem," the woman said. "We have to protect each other out here." The woman checked for cars, then ran across the road, and Allie followed her.

Once across the street, Allie picked up sight of Stan again. Although he had a fifty-pace lead on her, Stan didn't seem like he was walking with a purpose, more like he was taking a leisurely stroll through the city.

When they got to the park dedicated to the New England Holocaust Memorial, Allie stopped at the entrance. Before her stood six glass square towers under which visitors could walk. Stan stopped underneath the fourth tower and pretended to read something. At the far end of the park, she saw Drake pacing back and forth. Allie pulled her phone from her pocket. She brought up the messaging app and sent a group text.

I'm at the entrance to the memorial. I can see you. He's not following me, he's following you.

She watched the phone screen, then little bubbles appeared, so she knew someone was responding. It was Drake.

What should we do? Should we come to get you?

Allie thought for a second, then responded. *No. You three split up, each one take a different route back to the hotel. I'll follow him.*

She looked up from her phone, and as soon as she did, Ingrid and Geneva stood, and the three left together. They were near the corner already, so once they were there, Ingrid made a left turn and disappeared around the corner. Geneva waited for the light, then turned right, and Drake continued on straight ahead.

Allie kept her eyes on Stan, and when he walked, she did too. When he got to the corner, he stopped, looked left, right, and straight, as if trying to decide which way to go, then continued straight on down Congress Street. When she got to the corner, she crossed the street and realized that she was right back at Faneuil Hall.

Allie had made it a half block from the hall when she sensed someone fall into step behind her.

"You know you stand out like a reject from the F.B.I., right?" Ingrid said.

Allie laughed. "Don't mock me. This is my secret disguise. It fooled you, didn't it?"

"Not for a second. Where is he?"

Allie pointed up the street. "A hundred yards ahead. Gray pants, gray sweater."

"Okay, I see him."

"Weren't we just here?" Allie asked when they stopped for a moment in front of a building. She looked up into the air and pointed. "Yep. Unicorn. Is it me, or does Boston involve walking around in a lot of circles?"

"It only seems that way. You won't think that tomorrow when we go up to Salem. It'll get us a little outside of this area, and you'll be able to see some different things."

Allie took a step, stumbled, staggered, and almost fell face down in the center of the Boson Massacre memorial. Ingrid reached over, caught her, and prevented Allie from falling.

"Are you okay?" Ingrid said. There was a concrete planter holding a small fir tree nearby, and Ingrid helped Allie over to the planter and boosted her up so she could sit. "You didn't answer me. Are you okay?"

"I'm...fine. I just lost my balance. That's all. Help me

down," Allie said.

"You shouldn't lie to me, Allie. I'm trying to help you. You're practically in tears. I'm going to get us an Uber to take us back to your hotel, okay? Don't answer. It wasn't a question, and I'm not giving you a choice, so just sit there and be quiet."

Allie did as she was told and waited in silence until a car pulled up. The driver rolled down the window and Ingrid stuck her head in. "I'm sorry. It's such a brief ride. My friend hurt her leg. Do you mind if I put her in the front?"

The driver nodded, then moved his personal items from the front seat to the back.

Ingrid returned to Allie, helped her off the planter, and got her in the car. Once everyone buckled in, the driver took off like a shot, and within five minutes, they were at the hotel. Ingrid helped Allie from the car, then Allie leaned on her friend's shoulder and let her guide her past the lobby and to the elevator bank.

"I hope Drake and Geneva are okay," Allie said. "I feel like I abandoned them."

"Oh, don't you worry about them," Ingrid said. "They're big kids, and they'll be fine."

The door dinged, slid open, and the two trekked down the hallway. Allie fished the keycard from her pocket, and a few seconds later, Ingrid plopped Allie on the bed like she was dropping off her luggage.

"Drop your pants, let me look at your leg," Ingrid ordered.

"Excuse me?" Allie said.

"You heard me."

Allie hesitated and unbuttoned her jeans and slid them under her butt. She tried to reach for the right leg but couldn't do it. Ingrid stepped over, grabbed one pant leg in each hand, and pulled off Allie's pants in one smooth motion, folded them, and set them on the dresser.

"Wow," Ingrid said, "you've got some really nice legs. Well, except for that knee. It looks swollen."

Allie locked eyes with Ingrid for a moment, blushed slightly, and looked down at her leg. Her knee was indeed swelling rapidly. It wasn't yet twice the size of the other knee, but it was getting there.

"I'm going to get you some ice, okay? Don't go anywhere," Ingrid said.

Ingrid went into the bathroom and came back out with the plastic ice bucket.

"Ice and vending are one floor up," Allie said as Ingrid left the room.

Ingrid was back in a flash. "You wouldn't have a resealable bag on you, would you?"

Allie pointed to the floor. "There's one in my backpack."

Ingrid checked through the backpack and found an empty, gallon-sized plastic bag. She filled it with ice, then handed it to Allie, who placed it gently on her knee.

"Ooh, that's cold. You think you could grab me a towel?"

Ingrid did, and Allie wrapped the ice bag in the towel, then reapplied it.

"I wonder how Geneva and Drake are doing," Allie said.

Before she even finished the sentence, Ingrid's phone dinged. She checked and gave the report. "Geneva's waiting outside for Drake, and he's just a couple of blocks away. They'll be here within ten minutes."

"Well, shoot," Allie said, "can I ask for one more favor?"

"Sure, anything."

"Can you help me slide into a comfortable pair of sweatpants? They're in the top drawer over there, blue ones that say 'honey' on the butt."

Ingrid smiled and turned toward the dresser.

CHAPTER THIRTEEN

Allie was shivering. In her dream, she was adrift on an ice floe that was ten feet in diameter and shrinking by the minute. Swimming laps around the floe were a colony of penguins. Although there were only a dozen birds circling around her, every time one of them passed, her anxiety level rose. As she watched, one bird flew out of the water and landed on its feet only five feet from her. Allie knew her birds, and she could tell by the black and white tuxedo it wore that it was a Magellanic penguin.

The bird waddled a foot toward her and squawked, but she wasn't as concerned about the two-foot-high bird as she was about the ice that was rapidly melting. She noticed simply by looking that the ice had shrunk by another foot. Allie figured she had five minutes at most before the ice was gone, and she'd plunge into the freezing water. Since she was wearing only a pair of black panties, a black sports bra, and a pair of black socks, she assumed she'd become frozen as a fish stick as soon as she submerged for the first time.

The penguin took another step and opened his mouth.

That's when Allie noticed that the penguin's mouth didn't contain papillae, but rows and rows of razor-sharp shark's teeth. The bird stepped forward again. Allie took an instinctive step back, slipped on the ice, and fell on her butt. She struggled to get up but got no traction from her socks. Her legs worked overtime trying to get purchase, but she kept losing her footing. Allie rolled over on her hands and knees, and she was about to push to her feet when she sensed the strange sensation of webbed feet on her bare back. She stopped moving and felt the beak push past her ear and open. Allie smelled the scent of digested fish coming from the penguin's mouth, and she looked over her shoulder in time to see the bird poise for the killing strike.

Allie shrieked and woke herself from her nightmare.

The yell surprised Ingrid, who was sitting in the easy chair reading a book. She dropped her book, jumped to her feet, and ran to Allie's bedside.

"Hey, Allie, are you okay?"

Allie opened her arms, and Ingrid moved in and embraced her. After the coldness in her dream, Ingrid's closeness was warm and safe.

"Yeah. Only a bad dream. I was on a shrinking ice floe surrounded by penguins with shark teeth. I was so cold."

"Probably has something to do with this." Ingrid slid the covers from Allie's legs and picked up the bag, which was filled with frigid water from the melted ice. She removed the plastic bag and returned the bedspread.

"It seemed so real," Allie said.

"Yeah. I've had dreams like that, ones that stay with you the rest of the day."

"I hope this one doesn't. How long have I been asleep?"

Ingrid checked the bedside table clock. "Almost an hour and a half. How are you feeling?"

"Better, I think. I need to use the bathroom."

Allie threw back the covers and swung her legs over the

side, setting her feet on the floor. She hesitated for a minute, worried that her knee would buckle, and she'd collapse to the floor the second she put any weight on it. She surprised herself when she stood tall, with nothing more than a slight ache. Allie limped into the bathroom and a few minutes later, limped back to the bed and sat on the edge.

"Where are Drake and Geneva?"

"They left for dinner about an hour ago. I imagine they'll be back soon."

Allie's stomach rumbled at the mention of food. "Have you eaten? I think the hotel has a restaurant we can eat at."

Ingrid put her hand on Allie's knee. "I'm sorry, I misspoke. I meant to say that they're out getting dinner for all of us. There's a pizza place that Geneva really loves, but the place doesn't deliver, so they had to go pick it up."

Allie's stomach rumbled again. "Good. I really like pizza. It's one of my favorites."

"Me, too."

They heard a knock on the door, and Ingrid rose to answer it. Geneva entered first with a canvas sack in each hand, followed close behind by Drake, carrying two pizzas. They made their way to the small, two-seat table in the corner of Ingrid's room, and Drake set the pizzas on the table. With a grunt, Drake moved the heavy table toward the center of the room so they could all sit around it. After he adjusted the two chairs they had, he disappeared into his room to get his chairs.

While Drake was rearranging the furniture, Geneva unpacked the bags. From one, she pulled three six-packs of Diet Coke, and from the other she produced a pack of paper plates, napkins, and a handful of silverware.

When everything was ready, Drake and Geneva took seats, and Ingrid and Allie joined them at the table.

"Thanks for getting dinner. I'm starving," Allie said. "What do we have here?"

Drake placed the pizzas so they were next to each other, and flipped open the tops. "You can have a boring one with pepperoni, sausage, mushroom, and onion, or you can have the slightly less boring barbecue chicken with onion and bacon."

"How about a slice of each?" Allie said. "And why are they boring?"

Drake reached for a plate and pointed it at Geneva. "Ask her. She wanted to get something called a seafood special. I talked her out of it."

"Seafood? On a pizza? Yuck," Allie said as Drake passed her a plate.

Geneva shrugged. "No worse than pineapple on a pizza."

"I like pineapple on pizza," Ingrid and Allie said at the same time. They looked at each other, smiled, and giggled like teenagers.

Drake folded a slice of the barbecue chicken pizza in half and took a bite. He chewed a few times and nodded, as if he were agreeing most heartedly with a point someone made. He swallowed and took a drink of Coke. "Oh my, that's a good pizza," he said a second before he moved in for a second bite.

"I told you so. Best in town. Worth the trip and the wait," Geneva said. "How are you doing, Allie?"

Allie swallowed the bite she'd been eating and wiped her mouth with a napkin. "Much better, thanks. The rest did me a world of good. I'm sorry to you all that I had to give up my end of the pursuit."

Drake shook his head. "Don't worry about it. Splitting up was actually a good idea that you had. We all made a bad assumption that he had the hots for you, but it turns out I'm the one he's interested in."

"Are you sure? Did he follow you the entire way back?" Allie asked. "He never veered off, or kept on walking, or headed in a different direction?"

"Nope, he tailed me the entire time. At one point I slowed

down, and he didn't and came within twenty yards of me. Once that happened, it was easy to keep him spotted."

"How did you do that? Do you have eyes in the back of your head?" Geneva asked.

"No. I used this." Drake dug into his pants pockets and took out two items: a pair of tweezers, and a compact mirror. "No good geocacher leaves home without them. I tracked him in the mirror. He followed me all the way back to the hotel."

"Perhaps he was headed to his bookstore," Ingrid said.

Geneva shook her head. "Nope. The hotel is out of the way. He took the long route if he intended to go to his shop."

"But why would he follow Drake and not Allie?" Ingrid asked. "It was Allie who went to his store, and it was Allie he was making lovestruck eyes at yesterday. Why Drake?"

The room fell silent as everyone considered the question while they ate, but no one could come up with any logical or illogical answer to the question.

Allie finished her third slice of pizza, picked up a second napkin, and thoroughly wiped her hands and mouth. She crumpled the napkin into a little ball and placed it on top of her plate. "Okay, I've got another question for you all. We've been following these clues for the last couple of days, and what I don't understand is why all the hassle? Why bother going through the trouble of setting up all these convoluted clues in these random locations? Why not just have one cipher somewhere that tells the last location of the treasure, complete with a little X that marks the spot?"

Drake pushed his plate aside as well. "I've been thinking about that myself, and the conclusion I've come to is that I do not have a clue. Maybe it was a way to obscure the trail. It's possible there were only one or two people who had the treasure's hiding spot, and they backtracked it. You get it? They hid the treasure somewhere and told someone to hide a clue to get there. Afterwards, they got someone else to make a clue to find the previous person's clue. That way not everyone realized where it was, but everyone contributed to the elaborate scheme to hide it."

"Or more likely, it was a giant ruse to get the British to spend time and effort trying to track down a secret treasure that never existed," Geneva said.

"That could be as well," Drake admitted.

"Or it's all an elaborate fairy tale," Ingrid said.

"Could be that too," Drake said.

"What's the book say?" Geneva asked.

"Which book?"

"Which book? Come on, Drake, the book that started this whole baffling adventure. What does it say? Are we on the right track? Are the places we've been to even in the book?" Allie said.

"I'm not sure. I'll go get it," Drake said.

Drake disappeared into his room and returned a minute later, carrying his backpack. He placed it on the floor, opened it up, and rifled through it. He pulled out two empty water bottles and placed them on the table and underneath those found the book. In the process of putting the book on the table, he knocked the bottles, and they fell to the floor and bounced away.

Drake took a drink of Diet Coke, shook the can to confirm it was empty, and set it on the table. He opened the cover, then in dramatic fashion for the enjoyment of the others, he licked his finger and turned the page. He started reading, then started scanning the pages, flipping through them in a hurry, and skipping large chunks of information. Finally, he pushed the book across the table.

"Engaging reading?" Geneva said as she picked up the book.

"From what I can tell, it's mostly rumors and theories. Paul Revere is in there, but not a word about William Dawes. They mentioned the Old North Church, and Bunker Hill, Faneuil Hall, the USS *Constitution*, but only just in passing."

Geneva picked up the book and started going through it.

"That wasn't much of a book report. I'm sure Ingrid wouldn't give you a good grade on that one. What do you think? A 'D'?"

Ingrid smiled. "D-plus, at best. Could have been a C if he pronounced Faneuil correctly."

Geneva slowly paged through the book. "Okay, according to this, John Adams and Samuel Adams had the brainchild of hiding the treasure to prevent it from falling into British hands. From what this says, George Washington himself decided where to hide it, and sent Paul Revere to pass the message."

"If the treasure was so valuable, why not simply take it with them?" Ingrid asked. "You know, when Washington left town and started moving his headquarters farther and farther down the east coast? Clearly, he had the troops to make it happen."

Geneva shrugged without looking up and kept reading. "There are several theories in here, but all of them seem to agree that they buried the treasure on an island in the Atlantic Ocean. However, where the island is seems to be anywhere from the coast of Gloucester in the north to Martha's Vineyard in the south, and about a dozen points in between."

"Is there any information at all in there to narrow it down?" Allie asked.

Geneva continued through the last few pages, then closed the book and passed it back to Drake. "I don't think so. Even by my amateur eye, it seems to contain a lot of conjecture and a fair amount of sloppy research."

"How can that be?" Allie asked. "I thought that Hailey person we met with is one of the premier authorities on the American Revolution this side of the Mississippi. And she's on here as the co-author. You would think with all the documentation she has at her fingertips; she could figure this thing out without an issue."

"I don't know," Drake said. "I still think we're missing something on that end, but I don't know what. Either way, what about going to Salem tomorrow?"

"That depends. Are we going as tourists, geocachers, or treasure hunters?" Geneva asked.

Drake looked across the table. "Allie? What do you say?"

Allie got out her phone and checked her geocaching app. "It looks like there are four virtual caches up there, and a handful of traditional caches. Have y'all done any of these?"

"I haven't," Geneva said. "Have you done any caching up there, Ingrid?"

Ingrid shook her head. "No."

"Alrighty then. It looks like some of these caches correspond with historical locations anyway, so we'll go as geocachers first, tourists second. If we accidentally run into anything that would give us the next step to the treasure, then we'll do that," Allie said. "Oh, and lunch. We need to stop for lunch. How long will it take us to get up to Salem?"

"On a perfect day, a half hour. On a usual day, maybe an hour. All depends on how bad traffic is," Geneva said.

"Why don't we do breakfast at seven and try to be on the road by eight? Is that too early?" Drake asked.

No one objected.

"Next concern," Drake said as he stared down Allie. "Are you going to be okay, or should we take a rest day and hang out by the pool?"

Allie rolled her eyes at him in the most mocking manner she could. "I'll be fine. We'll have a car tomorrow, right? So, if I get tired, or the knee acts up, I'll just hang back and take it easy. It would also be helpful if we didn't do what amounts to a death march tomorrow."

"Okay, so what do y'all want to do with the rest of tonight?" Drake asked. He looked from Allie to Ingrid to Geneva, but no one spoke. "We could play cards. Or go to the movies. Or just hang out."

"What about the club? Why don't we go dancing?" Allie asked.

"Are you serious?" Drake asked.

Allie laughed. "Of course not, you goofball. Actually, I'd just like to curl up with a book and get some rest. That way I'll be ready for tomorrow."

"I get it," Drake said. "I'm good if we call it an early night."

Drake looked down at the pizza. "You want the leftovers with you?"

"Nah, you can have it," Allie said.

Drake consolidated the remaining five slices into one box and closed it. "I'll put it in my room fridge. If you get hungry during the night, just knock on the door and I'll slide a slice under."

Allie smiled. "That's so nice of you. Don't worry, I'll be good."

"Okay. Party's over. Geneva, can you help me with the chairs?"

Drake and Geneva each grabbed a chair that belonged in Drake's room and carried them through the door. While they were gone, Allie and Ingrid cleaned up the used plates and napkins and dumped them into the empty pizza box. While Ingrid took the trash and removed it from the room, Allie put the clean plates and napkins into a sack. She withheld a couple of cans of soda and put the rest in the other sack, then looked around. Satisfied everything was in order, Allie took a seat.

Drake came back into the room and gave Allie a hug. "I'm sorry about your knee. I still feel bad about that, you know."

Allie hugged him back. "You really shouldn't. I was the one who was careless on that hill, and I'm the one who has to pay the piper. I just need to accept the fact that I need to slow down for a while and try not to be super-woman all the time."

"Hey, I can help by not pushing you so hard, but you know how I get when I have a goal in sight. I just can't help myself."

"I know. That's how you always end up with briers on your pants, poison ivy on your hands, and random bloody holes from thorn encounters. You never look before you leap, but that's okay. We balance each other out that way."

"We do," Drake said. He released the hugs and grabbed the sacks. He said goodnight, then stepped through the door into his own room.

"Are you sure you two are just friends? You seem much closer than that," Ingrid said as she stepped back into the room.

Allie turned and smiled at her. "We are close. But just friends. I think I told you a long time ago that he's not my type."

"What is your type?" Ingrid asked as she moved closer.

Allie reached out her hand, and Ingrid took it. "To be honest, I prefer blondes. Preferably smart ones, with a good sense of humor. Oh, and someone who's easy to talk to."

"Anything else?" Ingrid asked as she took a step closer.

"Hmm. Sparkling blue eyes. A kind heart."

"You have quite a laundry list of expectations," Ingrid said. "I'm not sure that person exists in real life."

"I think they do," Allie said.

Ingrid took a step closer and wrapped her arms around Allie. "Are there any other qualifications?"

Allie smiled. "A good kisser. They need to be a good kisser. Are you a good kisser?"

Ingrid batted her sparkling blue eyes and whispered into Allie's ear. "Kiss me and find out for yourself."

CHAPTER FOURTEEN

"Is this a traditional or a virtual?" Ingrid asked.

Geneva checked the app. "It's a virtual. We need to either take a photo showing ourselves with the stones in the background, or—"

Drake interrupted Geneva in mid-sentence. "Hold that or, darling. I'm not sure why anyone would ever go beyond the photo part and actually do the task. The photo is so easy to take. Snap one shot, and you're done!"

"Not everyone likes to post a picture of themselves on the Internet, you know," Geneva said.

"True, but it's not like you're posing nude or anything. And most people post nothing besides selfies, anyway."

Geneva shook her head and snuggled close to Drake and snapped a picture with him. "There. Satisfied?"

She showed him the picture, and when he nodded his approval, she sent it to him and logged the geocache as a find for herself. "You guys want a picture, too?" she asked Ingrid and Allie.

"No. I'm already done with this one," Ingrid said, "and Allie seems preoccupied."

Geneva looked to her left and noticed Allie studying the nineteen names engraved into stones. "Allie? You want a photo for the cache requirements?"

Allie looked up from the marker she was reading. "No thanks. I took care of that the minute we got here. Can you imagine hanging nineteen people here for being witches? I mean, with no evidence other than the wayward claims of young girls? I can't wrap my brain around that."

"Well, it was three-hundred years ago. Definitely a different time," Geneva said.

"How did people let that happen?" Allie asked.

"I don't know," Geneva answered. "I'm sure when we get to the museum, someone could probably answer that question for you."

"Drake, do you think… what are you doing?"

Everyone turned their attention to Drake, who was looking at his phone and comparing it to the markers. "I'm looking to see if any of these people had the initials G.C., like what we found in the crypt yesterday."

Geneva passed her gaze quickly along the stones. It only took a few seconds to determine no one there had those initials. "I don't see a match."

Drake frowned and shoved his phone back into his pocket. "I didn't either."

"Wouldn't matter if you did," Ingrid said. "You wouldn't find any treasure clues here."

Drake looked up. "How do you know?"

Ingrid pointed to a small sign nearby. "Because they did not dedicate this park until 2017. I doubt the patriots would have had the foresight to hide clues in a location that wouldn't have a memorial until two hundred years later."

"Okay, that's a valid point."

"Besides, we're treasure hunters third today, remember?"

Geneva said. "Let's get in the car and move on to the next geocache. It's only a half mile from here."

They all got back in the car, and Geneva drove a few blocks, found street parking, and they all got out again. Drake checked his app and pointed to a stop sign fifty feet ahead of them. "I'll bet it's there," he said.

The four walked to the corner, and Drake checked all over the sign and the pole from as high as he could reach to the ground. Despite his search, he had no luck in finding it. He was about to give up when Ingrid handed him a small plastic box meant for hiding spare keys.

"Where was it?" he asked as he slid open the box and removed the paper log.

"Over there, behind the downspout attached to that building. You only missed it by less than fifteen feet," Ingrid said.

Drake signed the log and passed the sheet to the other three, and Ingrid put the geocache back together and returned it to where she found it.

Five minutes later, they parked outside of a three-story white mansion.

"Cool house," Allie said.

"Wait until you discover the garden around back," Geneva answered as she turned off the engine. "Unless plants aren't your thing, and in that case, we can grab the cache and leave."

"I'd vote for cache and go," Drake said.

"Me, too," Ingrid agreed.

"Okay, okay, I'll come back and enjoy the flowers on my own. This is another virtual. We need to find the sundial in the garden. The gnomon points to an information sign, and we need to grab the fifth word from the second sentence on the sign."

"What's a gnomon?" Drake asked.

"I think it's the pointy part of the sundial," Geneva answered. "Let's go find out."

The four walked into the maze. While Geneva stayed a step

behind to take pictures of the vegetation, the other three quickly found the sundial. Sure enough, the point of the sundial led to the sign with the answer they needed.

For their next stop, they visited the statue of Roger Conant, who was the person credited with founding the community of Salem. Together, they took a group photo for the requisite picture and logged the virtual geocache. Afterwards, Drake pointed to the large brick building across the street that resembled an old Gothic cathedral.

"Can we go over there?" Drake asked.

"The Salem Witch Museum?" Allie clarified. "Sounds fun, let's do it."

The quartet headed across the street and stepped into the museum. Lucky enough to secure a spot, they passed through the presentation that gave an in-depth examination of the Salem witch trials in 1692. They spent an hour going through the museum, then left the building and found a seat on the bench.

"Did you see what I did?" Drake asked.

"Um, like the history of the witch trials?" Allie answered.

"No. I think I figured out who G.C. is. Giles Corey, the dude who got pressed to death."

"Okay, I'd have to admit, that's a pretty good guess. What do we know about him?" Geneva asked.

"Other than a pressing was the grossest thing I would ever imagine? Not much. I'll find some info on him," Ingrid said as she pulled out her phone. As the others watched the tourists wander back and forth, Ingrid dug up all she could find on Giles Corey. After ten minutes, she set the phone on her lap and turned to the others.

"Well?" Drake asked.

"I found nothing we didn't already learn from the presentation we just saw. Originally from England, married three times, accused of being a wizard. During the trials, they pressed him to death when he didn't plead either guilty or not guilty to the charges against him."

"I don't suppose he's got a house around here that was perfectly preserved as a historical site," Drake said.

"Nope," Ingrid said.

"Did you find out where they buried him?"

"Sure," Ingrid said. "In an unmarked grave in what is now the Howard Street Cemetery. You'll be happy to know that it's rumored his ghost haunts the cemetery."

Drake leaned forward so he could hear Ingrid better over the din of the crowd. "And why would that make me happy?"

Ingrid grinned. "We simply go there tonight, and you can ask him all the questions you have about him."

Drake laughed. "That's a great idea, but I doubt he'd be able to tell me what clues people may have planted eighty years after he died. Is there anything else that connects him physically to the area?"

"No. Only a marker over at the memorial. That's all I found. I'm sorry," Ingrid dropped her head, and Allie leaned over and rubbed her shoulder.

"There's no need to be sorry," Drake said. "It's not your fault. If there's not a lot of information out there, then there's nothing you can do. Why don't we go over to the memorial? It's sounds touristy."

"Would you like to walk or drive over there?" Geneva asked.

"How far is it?" Drake asked.

Ingrid picked up her phone and mapped it out. "Three-tenths of a mile."

"Allie? Are you up for the hike? You're the only one who gets a vote."

Allie glanced from Drake's face to Ingrid's to Geneva's. "I'm kind of torn. On one hand, I'm afraid I'll injure myself again, but on the other, I'd really like to stretch my legs. I'm leaning toward walking."

"Let's do that. And if I need to go back to the car and pick you up, that's not a problem for me," Geneva said.

"Thanks. Okay, Ingrid, lead the way."

Ingrid got up from the bench, brushed off the seat of her jeans, got her bearings, and started walking. Although their destination was only a five-minute walk away, Ingrid walked at a slow pace. She made a show of looking at the architecture of buildings as they passed them.

"Are you moving like a snail for my benefit?" Allie asked as she slid into step next to Ingrid.

Ingrid glanced over and smiled without stopping. "Would I do that?"

"Probably."

Ingrid grew silent and kept the same gait of her stroll.

"Is there something on your mind?" Allie asked. "You've seemed kind of distant today."

"No. I just have some things on my mind. Plural," Ingrid said.

Allie stepped closer and lowered her voice. "I just asked you that. Did you hear me? Is it anything about last night?"

"Yeah, I guess."

"We can talk about it. You don't need to hide from me, Ingrid."

"No, it's not that. It's just… complicated. And I want to talk to you about it, but I need to wrap my head around what it is I want to say, so I can say it without sounding like an idiot."

"You wouldn't sound like an idiot. I won't judge you that way," Allie said.

"I know, but I'd also prefer if we talked when it was just the two of us. I have a feeling I won't get any guff from Geneva or Drake, but…"

"…but you don't want an audience. I can understand that. We can talk by ourselves whenever you feel that you're ready. Okay?"

"Okay. Thank you for understanding," Ingrid said.

"What are you two whispering about?" Drake asked.

"I get your point," Allie said to Ingrid. Allie stopped, turned around, and waited for Drake and Geneva to catch up to them. "We were talking about you."

"Oh yeah? About how I'm the greatest guy around? Besides being the world's greatest geocacher?"

Allie rolled her eyes. "Yep, that was it exactly. I was telling her about the time you were looking for that cache at the only probable location in a one-hundred-foot area."

"Oh? Did he have trouble finding it?" Geneva asked.

"He sure did. Drake lifted the light pole skirt and didn't find it. He stepped to the other side of the pole, lifted it again, couldn't find it. Then gave up. It turned out to be a fake electrical cover attached to the pole with magnets. I had spotted it right away, but he was so focused on assuming it was under the skirt, he looked nowhere else. He logged it as a DNF and then got mad at me when I walked right to it and slid it right off the pole."

"I think I see the memorial up ahead. Let's keep moving," Drake said as he pretended not to hear the conversation.

Allie smirked, then turned back around and kept walking. After another fifty feet, they arrived. The memorial was rectangular, and on each of the one-hundred-foot-long sides were four-foot-high stone walls. Attached to the walls were twenty granite benches. Etched into each bench was the name, means of execution, and execution date of a victim of the trials. A grassy patch and several large locust trees made up the middle of the memorial.

The four walked up the dirt path and reflected on the names carved into the granite. They passed the first ten benches without spotting the one they were searching for, then started down the other end of the rectangle.

Drake stopped when he finally found it. "Giles Corey. Pressed to death, September 19, 1692. Amazing, isn't it?"

"Sure is," Geneva said.

"I would have loved to learn more about him," Allie said.

"We could give Hailey a call. Maybe she could tell us something," Geneva suggested.

"Nah, I would think this might be outside of her area of expertise," Drake said.

"Excuse me, do you mind if I squeeze in here?"

Drake turned to look at the speaker. Before him was a man in jeans, a brown windbreaker, and a brown herringbone flat cap that matched the color of his jacket.

"I'm sorry. I wouldn't normally be this rude, but I'm on a deadline and I need to get some photos snapped of the benches," the man explained as he held up his Nikon for his credentials.

"No problem," Drake said as he stepped back from the bench. Ingrid and Geneva followed suit to give the man room, and Allie was already reading the details of the next victim.

The photographer looked into the viewfinder, then brushed away some grass from the top of the bench. Satisfied, he snapped the photo.

"Thanks again. Oh, and I didn't mean to eavesdrop, but if you're looking for anything about Giles Corey, there's an art gallery a block down Charter Street. They specialize in objects related to the witch trials. They might help you out."

"Thanks. We'll go down there for a look," Drake said.

The photographer moved on to the next bench, and Drake turned to the group. "Well? What do you say?"

"If it's only a block down, we might as well take a gander," Geneva said.

The four finished looking at the remaining benches, then left the memorial. Within three minutes, they were standing inside the art gallery.

"Can I help you?" the gallery owner asked as he came out from a back room. He looked right at home in the area where the witch trials took place, since the man resembled a witch himself.

He wore a black suit, black shirt, and a black tie. On his feet were black shoes, and on top of his head was a mop of raven-black hair. He even painted his fingernails black. The only trace of color on him was a lapel pin of a red rose.

"Yes, we're interested in seeing any pieces you may have about Giles Corey," Geneva said.

"I have a few prints of some of the more famous etchings of the time, like him being accused, or one of his pressing."

"Just prints? You have nothing original?" Drake asked.

"No. Sorry. I don't think anyone does from back then. It's not like it was a well-known event during that time. And once the trials were all over, the town tried their best to put that nasty piece of history behind them."

"Do you have anything from later, like maybe dating back from the 1700s?" Geneva asked.

The man in black looked at Geneva, as if trying to size her up. After two minutes of silence, he finally spoke. "I have one item, but it's not for sale. It's in my private collection."

"Can we see it? Pretty please? We won't be more than a moment."

The man considered it for a bit, then nodded. "I'll be back in a few minutes. Browse the shop while I'm gone if you wish."

Allie went off to get a closer look at the art on the walls, but the other three stayed clustered together, and within ten minutes, the man came back pushing a wood cart. A silver ewer protected by an acrylic box was on the cart. The man stopped near the group, and when Allie came back over, the man spoke.

"Paul Revere himself created this item. It's a solid silver ewer. It was a commissioned piece, and you can see engraved upon it, the pressing of Giles Corey."

"For real? Revere made this?" Geneva asked.

The man nodded. "I have the provenance on the paperwork going all the way back to 1775, including the sketches Revere made before he started the work."

"That's amazing. Can we see that?" Drake asked.

The man shook his head. "I'm sorry. It's not in the gallery. I keep the documentation in an off-site storage facility to keep it safe."

"I'm surprised you keep the ewer here," Geneva said.

The man smiled. "It's much too beautiful to be locked away." He looked beyond them when the door opened, and a couple entered the shop. "Please excuse me, I'll be right back."

"Keep a close eye on him and let me know when he's coming back," Drake said as he took out his phone. With as much haste as he could muster, he snapped photos of the ewer from all four sides. Once he finished, Drake stowed his phone back into his pocket and resumed the stance of a casual observer.

"It's a remarkable piece, isn't it?" Drake asked Geneva when he noticed the man coming back toward them.

"It is," Geneva agreed. "I've seen nothing like it anywhere before."

"Well, what do you think?" the man asked.

"Beautiful. Why isn't it in a museum?" Allie asked.

The man grinned. "Pure selfishness on my part. I couldn't stand the thought of it being out of my possession for even a moment. Is there anything else I can help you with?"

Drake shook his head, and as the man pushed the cart back from where he got it, the four left the gallery. They walked up the block, then Drake spotted a bar and grill with outdoor seating. "Anyone hungry?"

Every one of the three women replied in the affirmative, so they went to the tavern and got a table outside under an umbrella. They took a moment to examine the menu before ordering drinks and burgers, and once that bit of business was out of the way, Drake passed his phone over to Allie.

"Can you look at the pictures and see what you can see?"

Allie took the phone and started scanning through the photos. She took her time and enlarged each one as she looked through them. She hadn't finished by the time the server arrived with burgers for all, so Allie passed Drake's phone back to him, and the four settled into small talk as they ate.

A few blocks away, while the four friends were busy enjoying lunch, Stanford Edison stepped into the art gallery. He wasn't usually a patron of the arts, but he was interested in knowing why Drake and his friends had been there.

CHAPTER FIFTEEN

After Allie finished her burger, she pushed her plate aside, wiped her mouth and fingers with a napkin and asked Drake for his phone. Drake handed it back over, and Allie continued looking through the pictures.

"Are you seeing anything?" Drake asked. He dipped an onion ring into a puddle of ranch dressing while he waited for the answer.

"I'm working on that," Allie said. "If there is anything here, it's pretty well hidden."

"There has to be something. I can't believe that someone would really get Paul Revere to create that ewer with such an odd subject," Geneva said.

"I would love to find out who commissioned the piece. Perhaps it would tell us something to know who the piece went to," Ingrid said.

"Yeah, that would have been nice," Drake said as he finished the last bite. "All we would need to do is go back into the gallery and demand that he show us the documentation."

"Or we could go all ninja and break into the storage place and get the records ourselves," Geneva said.

"Did he mention where it was?" Drake asked.

Geneva grabbed her iced tea and took a sip. "I was being sarcastic. You may have noticed that although each of us brings a particular set of skills to the table, none of us are cat burglars."

"We don't need to go back," Allie said. "Anyone have a pen?"

Allie knew it was a rhetorical question because all geocachers carried a pen, sometimes even when they weren't geocaching. She herself had a half dozen of them in her backpack, but she was too lazy to go digging for them. Instead, she took the first one to appear in front of her, which turned out to be Ingrid's. The server left a stack of extra paper napkins on the table, so Allie took the one off the top. She unfolded the napkin and started copying symbols from the pictures to the napkin.

"What did you find?" Drake asked.

Allie ignored the question until she finished jotting down the symbols. "Clever of old Paul. He engraved these in the bottom edge of the ewer, made to seem like a decorative border." She expanded the photo she was referring to and held the phone so everyone could examine the picture. "See? I'm positive that's a code."

"How can you tell?" Geneva asked.

"The border doesn't repeat. Usually when you see a border around anything, it's a repeating pattern, right? It's human nature to want a sense of evenness, and this border doesn't have it. It's unnatural."

Ingrid asked for the phone and looked closer at the pictures. "I think you're right."

Drake motioned for his phone back, then slipped it into his pocket. "She usually is. The next logical question is, can you break the code? I mean, all I spot are random symbols, and if you say there's a code hidden in that base, then there is. The question is, how do you break the thing?"

"We could start by taking a picture of it and seeing if any of the symbols pop up in an image search online," Geneva suggested.

"That's a good idea," Allie said. She passed the napkin over to Geneva, who took several photos of it, then gave the napkin back. "In the meantime, I'll try to break the code the old-fashioned way. Trial and error."

Allie put the napkin down and stared at the symbols for a moment, then took a fresh napkin and made a copy of the first. Once she had a backup, she leaned over and tapped the pen on the table while she inspected the napkin. All the symbols were etchings of animals. On a third napkin, Allie copied a symbol, then wrote the number of times it repeated next to the symbol. There were two different snakes, one facing left, the other right, and each had a count of ten. She made out two bird heads, one with a short beak, one with a long beak, both of which had two instances. Allie recognized a turtle, which showed up twice, and a frog, which had only one entry.

"I think we have only four letters here, based on the repeating images," Allie said.

"How do you figure that?" Drake asked.

Allie pointed at the snakes. "There are too many instances of these to be letters. I think they are just here to take up space." She grabbed another napkin and rewrote the symbols, leaving the snakes off of the napkin. When she finished, there were only seven symbols left.

"There's only one non-repeating letter in here, the frog. One letter has two instances, but not doubled, and two places where I think are double letters. Ingrid, can pull up one of those word finder apps?"

Ingrid fussed with her phone for a minute. "Okay, got one. Give me some parameters."

"Hold on. Let's assume that the first letter is a consonant, and the second and fifth letters are vowels. Then there are two separated double letters. Seven letters only. Hold on. Let me see if I can map this out. Can you pull me up a list of common repeating letters?"

Ingrid made a query and had the answer in an instant. "The most common repeating letters are E, L, S, O, T, F, R, N, P, and C."

"What about at the end of a word?"

Ingrid worked for almost thirty seconds to get the information. "E, L, S, and F."

"I'm going to guess that is an L or S at the end. The E wouldn't make sense."

"If you're knocking out the E as a double, I'd get rid of the O as well. What does that leave us with?" Geneva said.

Allie checked her scratching. "Starting with A, blank, A, L, L, A, S, S. Does that mean anything to anyone?"

No one said a word.

"Okay, how about blank, A, S, S, A, L, L?"

"'Assall'? That doesn't sound like anything," Drake said.

"You need to put a letter in front. Like a C to get 'cassall', or G to get 'gassall'."

Drake waved his hand at Allie. "Yeah, but those aren't words."

Ingrid smiled, as if a light bulb came on. "Yeah, but if you add a V, you get vassall. There's a name I've heard before, but I can't remember where. Give me a second." She checked for a hunch. "Got it. The Vassall House is where George Washington had his first headquarters in 1775."

"Any chance it's still standing?" Geneva asked.

"Not only is the building still standing, but it's now a part of the National Park Service. It's in Cambridge."

"Where's that from here?" Drake asked.

"Back toward Boston, about an hour from here," Geneva answered. "You want to go for a drive, don't you?"

Drake looked at her, then gave her a smile. "It is a historical site, right?"

"It is," Ingrid said. "Not only did Washington use the house as his headquarters, but Longfellow owned it as well."

"Longfellow the poet?" Allie asked.

"Yep."

"That is interesting. I'm in if you guys are," Allie said.

Geneva smiled. "Okay. Let's go get the car and hit the road."

An hour in the mid-afternoon traffic took an hour and a half, but eventually Geneva found her way to Cambridge and parked in front of the Longfellow house. The house was a three-story mansion, painted yellow with a large white door, white window trim, and black shutters. There was a large yard in front, and the quartet walked up the front sidewalk and stood before the house's door.

Drake took off his hat, scratched his head, and put his hat back on. "Looks too good for being so old. They must have rebuilt it at some point."

Geneva pulled on Drake's arm to move him along. "Let's go find out."

"Welcome to the Longfellow House," the park ranger said as the friends entered the visitor center. "Are you interested in a tour?"

Drake stepped forward to represent the group. "Sure. Could you tell us a little about the house's history first?"

"Of course. As you can see from the outside, they built the

house in the Georgian style in 1759 for John Vassall, Jr., who used the home as a summer residence. In 1774, patriots confiscated the house, and General George Washington used it from 1775 to 1776 as his house and headquarters. The house passed through various hands after the war. Ultimately, poet Henry Wadsworth Longfellow received it as a wedding gift from the father of his new bride Frances Appleton. After his death, the surviving Longfellow children put the house into a trust in 1913, and in 1972 the trust donated the property to the National Park Service."

"What's in the house now?" Geneva asked.

"Since the Longfellow family held the property for so long, the house is as when Henry lived and worked here. There's also an excellent exhibit based on some guests the Longfellow family had come through. The dignitaries included Charles Dickens, Ralph Waldo Emerson, and Oliver Wendell Holmes. The emperor of Brazil once visited as well."

"That all sounds cool, but we're primarily interested when Washington used the house as his headquarters. Are there any exhibits highlighting that era?"

"Yes. There is one room that was used as Washington's office when he was in the house that is set up the way we believe it was back then."

"Can we check out that one?" Drake asked.

"You're not interested in the rest of the house?" the ranger asked. "Usually when people visit, they want to experience what it was like in the time of the Longfellows."

"Oh, you see, our friends here are visiting from Nashville. They came all the way here to learn about the American Revolution. We wanted to show them something associated with General Washington," Geneva explained.

"You don't want to tour anything else, just the Washington room?"

"Not unless it was authentic to the time Washington was

here," Geneva clarified.

"Well, why don't you four follow me and I'll take you over," the ranger said.

"Are you sure you can leave your post? What if someone else comes in?" Allie asked.

The ranger smiled at her, then stood, and reached for his hat. "Not a problem. My partner should be back soon, and it won't take us long to see the one room."

He led the group from the visitor's center and locked up behind him. He led the party to the entry door of the mansion, and they stepped into the blue entryway. They walked directly through the front parlor and into a room dedicated to Washington's stay at the house.

Along one wall was a fireplace, and above the fireplace were portraits of George and Martha Washington. There stood a simple wood table underneath the lone window. Scattered on the tabletop were several maps and pieces of correspondence. On a mannequin in the corner was a reproduction of Washington's coat and hat, and a side table held a few old books.

"Not much to learn here," Drake said.

"That's why there's only the one room," the ranger explained. "When Washington left the house, they took pretty much everything with them when they moved on to the Dexter House in Dedham. What we have here is a basic recreation based on what few items we had from the time."

"Is there anything original?" Drake asked.

The ranger shook his head. "No, I'm sorry. Even the portraits are reproductions. If you want to see the originals, you'd have to go down to D.C."

Ingrid pointed at a framed hand-written document on the wall. "What's this?"

The ranger walked over to it and straightened the frame. "This is actually an original. A poem written by Phillis Wheatley entitled 'To His Excellency, George Washington' that she sent to

Washington himself in 1775. What you see on the wall there is what the *Pennsylvania Gazette* republished in 1776."

"I've never heard of Phillis Wheatley," Geneva said.

"I'm not surprised, although more people should. Historians consider Wheatley the first African-American author of a published book of poetry. She was born in West Africa, kidnapped, and sold as a slave. When she came to North America, the Wheatley family bought her. She learned to read and write and started writing poetry. After she published her first book, she got emancipated. Rumor has it she and Washington corresponded with each other several times, and newspapers published several more of her poems."

"What happened to her?" Ingrid asked.

"She died young and poor in Boston." The ranger's radio squawked, and he stepped out of the room to take the call.

"While we have a moment alone, look around and check if we missed anything important," Drake ordered.

The four split up and inspected everything in the room. Drake dedicated his effort to the fireplace. They looked for clues, but there was nothing to be found. Dejected, they left the room, walked out of the house, and found the ranger outside, still having a conversation over the radio.

The ranger spotted the group, waved at them, then headed back toward the visitor's center.

"Well? What now?" Geneva asked. "Should we do a loop around the exterior? Check out the carriage house?"

Drake scrunched his face and shook his head. "I don't know if it's worth it. I think we finally hit the end of the road here. So, with that, back to geocaching. Is there anything around here to find?"

Ingrid was the first to open her app and check. "There's an EarthCache and a multi-cache nearby. Those are the two closest.

Anyone interested?"

"You know I'm not a fan of EarthCaches," Allie said. "How hard does the multi look?"

Ingrid brought up the cache detail and checked it out. "Doesn't look too bad at all. Looks like stage one gets you the call number, and they hid the final inside of the library."

Allie's face brightened. "You should have led with that. I love library caches!"

Five minutes later, they were in the parking lot of the library, and were looking for stage one around the library's bulletin board.

Drake spotted it first. "I have it. It's 796.233."

"You sure?" Geneva asked.

Drake pointed at the sheet he was reading from. "They have a list of the most popular books of the month. One is titled *Finding Tupperware in the Woods* by G. Cacher."

Geneva nodded. "Good enough for me. Let's go in."

Drake held the outer door and let the ladies enter the library before him. As with entering any library for the first time, it took them a couple of minutes to get their bearings. It wasn't long until they headed for the 796 section of the stacks. Once there, all four of them scanned the shelves until Allie pointed at the book they needed.

Geneva pulled the volume from the shelf and opened the book. They had all seen geocaches in libraries before. Some were fake books; some were plastic containers hidden in book sleeves. The most common was the one they had before them. Someone had gone through the work of cutting a hole in the inner pages, leaving just enough on the edges to make it resemble an actual book. They glued the title page to a thin piece of cardboard, and when Geneva turned the page, they found the goodies inside. The contents included a green plastic army man, a pair of red dice, and a coupon for a free ice cream cone. Geneva pulled the paper log from inside and passed it around. Once everyone signed, she tucked it back into the book and returned the book to the shelf.

Together, they all left the section and headed toward the door. On the way out, Allie stopped when she got to a computer, hit the spacebar to activate the screen, and brought up the library catalog. Once she got in there, she did a name search on Phillis Wheatley, and found a grand total of one book in her name. She jotted down the Dewey Decimal number for the book on a scratch pad next to the computer and ripped the page from the pad. She turned to ask a question, but discovered all her friends were gone.

Allie shrugged, glanced at the note, and headed back to the stacks to find the American poetry section. When she got to the eight-elevens, she scanned the shelf but couldn't find the book she wanted. Allie took a step back, put her fingers on the book a few spots ahead of where she expected the volume to be, and touched each book in sequence to make sure she hadn't missed it. Once satisfied she hadn't just passed it over, she checked the shelf above where the book should have been. When that was unsuccessful, she checked the shelf below. There, in the American Drama section, was the book she wanted.

Allie opened the book and checked the table of contents. In there she noticed the same poem she saw hanging on the wall of the Longfellow House, and several others as well.

"There you are. Where did you disappear to?" Ingrid said as she appeared in the aisle. "Allie? Are you there?"

Allie looked up from the book, then closed it. "Sorry, what?"

"We got back to the car and realized you weren't there. Drake wanted to leave you behind, but I said I'd come in and look for you."

Allie grinned. "He's such a dork, isn't he? Hey, do you have a library card that works for this library?"

Ingrid held up her phone. "Sure. There's an app for that."

"Can you check out this book for me?" Allie handed the volume of poetry over to Ingrid, who took it and glanced at the spine.

Ingrid raised an eyebrow and held the book up. "What's this about? A little light reading?"

Allie smiled. "Just a hunch. Can you get it for me, pretty please?"

"I don't know. Checking out a book for someone else can be a dangerous thing. You never know if they will return it, and the next thing you know, you've racked up a dollar's worth of late fees and your card gets disabled."

"You're just as big of a dork as Drake is. Come on, let's get out of here before they really leave us behind."

CHAPTER SIXTEEN

It was a few minutes after eight, and Allie had settled into bed with the Phillis Wheatley book when she heard a gentle knock at her door. She threw the covers off her, plodded over to the door, and opened it, and discovered Ingrid standing there.

"I'm sorry. Hey, I get I should have called first, but I thought since I was nearby anyway, I'd stop by. I have a question for you."

"Sure, what is it?"

Ingrid smiled. "Would you like to meet my cat?"

"Your cat? I didn't know you had a cat. Want to come in?"

Without waiting for the answer, Allie backed away from the door to allow Ingrid room to enter. "Are you serious about me meeting your cat?"

Ingrid nodded. "I realize it seems silly."

"Is your cat here?"

"Of course not. She's back at my apartment. It looks like you're ready for bed. I'm sorry. I'll leave you be and catch you tomorrow."

Ingrid turned to leave, but Allie reached out and grabbed

her arm. "No, wait. I'd love to meet your cat. Give me a moment to get dressed."

Allie grabbed her jeans that were folded over the back of the chair, took off her sweats, and got into her jeans. She tucked her t-shirt into her pants and zipped them up. She grabbed her room key from the top of the dresser and slipped into her shoes.

"Okay, I'm ready. Lead the way," Allie said.

Forty-five minutes later, Ingrid slipped the key into the lock of her apartment door. "Watch out. She likes to make a break for it sometimes."

Allie took a step back and waited for a little ball of fur to rush her way the second that Ingrid opened the door a crack, but no cat appeared.

"And sometimes she doesn't." Ingrid stepped over the threshold and flipped a light switch.

There was a small bench next to the door in the entryway, and Ingrid slipped out of her shoes and tucked them under the bench. To be polite, Allie followed suit.

Ingrid walked into the living room and turned on another light. "Come on in and make yourself at home. I'll go find Roxie."

Allie sat down on the couch and looked around the room. There was a television set and three bookshelves, crammed with books, on the opposite wall from the couch. In front of the couch was a small coffee table holding a laptop, and in front of the balcony windows was a small easy chair. From where she sat, Allie could look at the area set aside as the dining area, which contained a small square table and two chairs, and a door she assumed led to the kitchen.

A shadow crossed the room and the next thing she knew, Allie's breath was knocked out of her chest as the largest cat she'd ever seen jumped into her lap. She tried to push the beast away, but instead, the cat reached up and put its paws over Allie's shoulder and nuzzled in her ear. The cat's purr was loud enough to make Allie believe she was on an airplane.

"Oh, you found Roxie!" Ingrid said as she came back into view.

"More like Roxie found me. I was expecting a house cat, not a full-grown tiger."

"She's part Maine Coon, part Russian Blue."

"She's gorgeous is what she is," Allie said as she petted the cat's slate gray fur. "Is she going to get any bigger?"

"Oh, I hope not. She's almost like having an elephant for a pet as it is. Here, let me take her from you."

Ingrid grabbed Roxie and with a grunt, lifted the cat and placed her on the chair. The cat stood, did a lazy circle, and laid down. Roxie put her head on her paws and closed her green eyes.

"Thanks for coming over. You want something to drink? Beer? Soda? Water?" Ingrid asked, mindful of being a good host.

"I'd take a glass of water, thanks."

"Ice?"

"No. Straight out of the tap is fine."

Ingrid traipsed into the kitchen and returned with two bottles of room temperature water and passed one over to Allie, opened the other, and took a drink.

Allie waited. She sensed Ingrid wanted to say something. She didn't, and instead, Ingrid played with the bottle cap and stared at her cat. "Everything okay, Ingrid?"

Ingrid turned her attention from Roxie and gave it to Allie. "Can we talk about last night?"

"Of course. What's on your mind?" Allie put her bottle on the floor and turned sideways in her seat, so she was facing Ingrid.

Ingrid looked from Allie to the floor, picked a spot on the carpet, and stared at it. "I wanted you to understand that I realized last night was really special. It was a first for me, for sure, and I didn't want you to think that I did it just because I think you're pretty. I really like you, and I've never had these feelings for anyone the way I feel them for you."

Allie reached over, placed her fingers beneath Ingrid's chin, and gently lifted her head to force her to make eye contact.

"Wait. You said I'm pretty?" Allie asked.

Ingrid hesitated and nodded.

"I think you're pretty, too. Beautiful, in fact. You should know that I've never felt this way before, either. I've been in quasi-relationships with both men and women, but never anything serious. I've never thought about wanting anything serious. At least, until I met you."

Ingrid took Allie's hand in hers. "I'm in love with you, Allie. Since the moment I first saw you last year."

Allie squeezed Ingrid's hand. "I love you, too."

Ingrid's face turned from uncertainty with a side of fear to exuberance in a heartbeat. "So now what?"

Allie leaned forward and gave Ingrid a gentle, lingering kiss. "I have no clue. You tell me."

The next morning, Allie's eyes fluttered open, and she was aware of three things. First was the sunlight peering in through the window. The second was the sensation of an enormous weight on her lower legs. The third, and best, were Ingrid's blue eyes looking at her.

"Good morning," Allie said. "How long have you been awake?"

"Only a few minutes. I wanted to glance at you to make sure last night wasn't a dream. Now that I say it out loud, that sounds super creepy."

Allie smiled. "No. Not creepy at all. Why can't I move? Did you drug me? Because that would be super creepy."

Ingrid laughed. "Nope, that never crossed my mind. You're sleeping on Roxie's side of the bed, and she decided that you're only a lumpy part of the mattress. Roxie, time to get up. Roxie, up."

Allie sighed when the blood came rushing back to her legs as the cat stood, stretched, and finally jumped down to the floor with a loud thump. She leaned over, gave Ingrid a kiss.

"I have to use the bathroom," Ingrid said. She threw off the covers, slid out of bed and padded off into the other room, naked.

Allie got out of bed, found her clothes, and got dressed while she waited for Ingrid to reappear. She heard the toilet flush, and the sink run for an extended time. When Ingrid finally appeared, she had brushed her hair and when she gave Allie a kiss, Allie tasted the fresh mint of Ingrid's toothpaste.

"Would you mind feeding Roxie while I get dressed? The food is in the cabinet next to the fridge, and her bowl is in the sink. Then I'll run you back to the hotel so you can get ready for the day."

Allie moved into the kitchen, had a drink of water, then found Roxie's dish. She found a can of chicken and rice cat food in the cabinet and dumped the contents into the bowl. Before she uttered the first syllable to call the cat, Roxie was at her feet, looking up at her. Allie put the bowl on the floor and let Roxie go to it.

"Ready to go?" Ingrid asked as she came out of the bedroom, ready to take on the day.

"Sure thing. What time are we meeting the others for breakfast?"

"Nine," Ingrid answered. "But you know how they are. It will be closer to ten before we get a peep from them."

Allie saw her phone and hotel key on the coffee table and retrieved them. She checked the phone and saw she had no text messages or missed calls overnight. She also noticed it was going on six-thirty.

Allie shoved the phone into her pocket. "Do you always get up this early?"

Ingrid pushed her way into the kitchen, checked the water level in Roxie's fountain, and topped off her bowl of dry food.

"Yeah, usually. I've always been an early riser. Is that a problem?"

"Not in the least. I'm the same way," Allie said.

By seven-fifteen, Ingrid and Allie were back in Allie's hotel room. While Ingrid watched the morning news, Allie took a quick shower, brushed her teeth, and got into fresh clothes.

"Okay, I'm ready to go," Allie announced as she zipped up her jeans. She checked her phone and saw it was not yet a quarter to eight. "Although I guess I'll sit for a bit. You want some coffee?"

Ingrid shook her head. "No thanks. I can't stand the stuff."

"Something else we have in common. So now I guess we wait until we hear from the others."

"I hope Geneva set an alarm. She could sleep all day if you let her."

Allie walked over to the nightstand where she'd left the Wheatley book the night before and carried it over to the table and sat. "There's something else she has in common with Drake. I can't tell you how many times we've been late to things because he has trouble getting out of bed. Want a Diet Coke?"

"Sure. Wait, I got it." Ingrid got up from the bed and retrieved the cans of Diet Coke they had saved from the night before and joined Allie at the table. "Mind if I sit with you?"

Allie opened a can and took a drink. "Of course, you can. Do you mind if I read for a while? I want to see if there's anything in this book that leads to the treasure."

"Go ahead. I can entertain myself."

Ingrid moved her chair so she could watch the television while Allie read. An hour and a half passed without either of the women saying a word. The only sounds in the room were the noise from the television and the sound of paper scraping across paper as Allie turned the pages.

"The fires of freedom from Boston burns. From Salem to Concord, from the Graveyards to the Steeples. From Houghs Neck to Hayman's, and again to Rainsford. Follow the march to Freedom's Ring."

Ingrid found the clicker and turned down the volume of the television. "Can you read that again?"

Allie repeated the passage she'd just read, then put a marker in the book and closed it.

"Okay? And? What's so special about those lines?" Ingrid asked.

"I don't accept Phillis Wheatley wrote that, even though a Boston paper published it under her name in 1775."

"Why not?"

Allie pushed the book toward Ingrid. "Read it. But before you do, read a few of the poems before, and a few after. I don't have a doctorate in literature, but I can tell the same person didn't pen those poems. You teach lit, right? Read them and tell me what your thoughts are."

Ingrid picked up the book and did as Allie suggested. It was Allie's turn to remain silent while Ingrid studied the pages. Rather than turn to the television or her phone to amuse herself, Allie sat patiently and waited for Ingrid to finish.

A half an hour passed before Ingrid put the bookmark back and set the book on the table. "You're right. There's no way that Wheatley wrote that poem. The tone and cadence and voice are all significantly different from any other work in the book. And it's certainly not as good as any of the other poems in there."

"And it doesn't rhyme," Allie pointed out.

"No, it did not."

"Now we need to ask, why would a newspaper print this poem, and attribute it to Wheatley, even though it clearly wasn't hers? Can you read it again? Aloud?"

Ingrid picked up the book, found the place, and read. "The fires of freedom from Boston burns. From Salem to Concord, from the Graveyards to the Steeples. From Houghs Neck to Hayman's, and again to Rainsford. Follow the march to Freedom's Ring."

"You've got a lovely reading voice," Allie said. "Boston to

Salem to Concord. Graveyards to church steeples. Any of that seem familiar to you?"

"You mean like the various places we've found clues?"

Allie took another drink. "Exactly. Now, what about the rest of it? Someone's neck, a hay man, and a dude named Rainsford? Are those more clues?"

"Houghs Neck isn't a body part. It's a land mass at the south end of Quincy Bay. Did you know they interred John Adams and John Quincy Adams and their wives in the same crypt in a Quincy church?"

"No, I didn't. We should stop by there if we have the chance. I'd love to see it. What about Hayman's? Is that a person?"

Ingrid did a bit of magic on her phone and quickly came up with the answer. "Hayman's is an island. Today it's called Hangman Island. It's a chunk of rock northwest of Houghs Neck. And before you ask, Rainsford is also an island in the bay."

"What do we know about that one?"

Ingrid looked it up. "In the olden times, the Native Americans used it. During the 1700s, settlers used the island for farming and cattle."

"Is that it then? Is that the last clue? Rainsford is the location of the treasure?" Allie asked.

"I don't think so. I imagine we're missing something else. Every other clue we found one at a time, so why list out three locations at once?"

"I don't know. Perhaps we need to get Geneva and Drake involved. I'm sure they can figure this out," Allie said.

Without waiting for a reply, Allie walked to the connecting door and knocked. Much to her surprise, Geneva opened the door right away.

"Hey, Geneva. Are you guys up?"

"For the most part. Drake is in the shower. Are you hungry already? Are we going to the pancake place for breakfast?"

Allie's stomach rumbled at the mention of pancakes. "I'd

love to, but I wonder if we found the next clue to the treasure. We think we're on to something but can't quite figure it out. We were hoping that you and Drake could look at what we found."

"Okay, sure."

Allie stepped back into her room, and Geneva followed her over to the table. Once Geneva settled into a chair, Allie explained her suspicions and Geneva took the book and read through the passages.

After a few minutes, Geneva set the book down. "I'm not saying you're wrong, but I don't see it."

"Surely you agree Wheatley didn't write the poem," Ingrid said.

Geneva gave a loud, long exhale. "I honestly couldn't tell you. But I'm not an expert on literature or 1700s poetry. All I can tell you is it didn't rhyme. It's probably just a coincidence and you're reading too much into it. What's that old saying, if all you have is a hammer, then everything you see is a nail? I just don't know. Maybe you should wait and get Drake's opinion."

"About what?" Drake asked as he came through the door, his hair still wet from the shower.

"Allie thinks she found a clue to the secret treasure in a poem published in a Boston newspaper for all to see," Geneva said.

Drake turned to Allie. "Really?"

Allie nodded.

"Show me what you got."

Allie passed Drake the book and had him read a few poems before pointing out the one of interest. While he read, the women watched him, and he glanced up several times while he was reading, a look of discomfort on his face. When he finished, he gave them his full attention. "I don't get what you're looking at."

Allie sat down on the bed and subconsciously rubbed her knee. "It's best if you take it one line at a time and compare it to where we've already been. Boston, Salem, churches, cemeteries, those are all written in the poem, right? Then you have those next three places, Houghs Neck and two islands. Surely that can't be a coincidence."

"Where are these located?" Drake asked.

Ingrid pulled out her phone and opened a map. "They're all close to Quincy Bay. Here, look."

Ingrid handed Drake the phone, and he studied it for a moment.

"I'm guessing the next three steps to the treasure are at those three points," Allie said.

Drake shook his head. "Why would they put three clues in one place when they've been so careful about doing them one at a time?"

Ingrid smiled. "That's the same thing I said."

Drake looked at the phone again, then stared at the ceiling for a full minute. He came out of his trance, then looked at the women. "Nobody move. I'll be right back."

Drake left the room, went through the door into his room, and a few seconds later, the exterior door to his room opened and closed.

"I guess we'll wait here," Geneva said.

Allie raised her hands above her head and stretched. "I hope he's not gone too long. You've got me thinking about those pancakes."

Ten minutes later, there was a knock at the door, and when Ingrid answered it, she found Drake on the other side.

"Sorry, I forgot my key." Drake made his way to the table and laid down three sheets of paper on the table, then adjusted them so they lined up the way he wanted them to. "I went down to the business center and printed out some enlarged maps of the areas listed in the poem."

Allie got up from the bed and joined the others, and Ingrid pointed out the three locations.

Drake took a pen from the bedside table. "I was thinking,

why three at once? Maybe because they needed three points." He grabbed the book, placed it on the paper, then used it as a straightedge to draw a line. He repeated the process twice more, then set the book aside. "What do you see now?"

"A triangle." Geneva said.

Drake drew a circle on the page. "Yeah. What's in the center?"

Geneva leaned in, then took the paper from the table and held it up. "It's an island."

CHAPTER SEVENTEEN

Allie poured warm maple syrup over her blueberry pancakes. Once she had the entire pancake covered in the gooey substance, she passed the bottle to Ingrid. Allie used her fork to cut off a wedge of pancake and ate it. She smiled as she chewed and happily swallowed.

"Oh, my, that's one of the best pancakes I've ever eaten," she said. "I assume these blueberries are fresh. Anyone want a bite?"

Everyone was engaged with their own breakfasts, so no one took her up on it. Ingrid had a plate of French toast in front of her. Geneva was working on a Denver omelet, and Drake had a plain plate with a couple of eggs over easy with a compliment of bacon, toast, and hash browns.

"There are two things we should probably talk about," Drake said as he mopped up some egg yolk up with a piece of bread. "First thing, we need to talk about the secret treasure. Should we go for it or should we not? Should we spend a day geocaching? Be normal tourists and go to a museum or something? What's the temperature of the room here? Everyone gets a vote today."

"What do you want to do?" Geneva asked.

Drake dabbed at his mouth with a napkin. "Nope. No, no, no, no. I'm not saying. In fact, here's an idea." Drake pulled a small notepad from his back pocket and ripped out a page. "Everyone, take a sheet and write your preference. The option with the most votes wins."

Drake passed the pad around and everyone ripped out a page.

"What if there's a tie?" Ingrid asked.

"If it's a tie, we have the server do a blind pick. Fair enough?"

Drake produced a pen, recorded his choice, folded the paper in half, and passed the pen to Geneva. Geneva took the pen, hid the paper as she cast her vote, and sent the pen to Ingrid. Ingrid let the pen and the paper sit where they were until she finished eating the rest of her breakfast. When she finished the last bite of her toast and had a drink of orange juice to wash it down, Ingrid pushed her plate to the side, picked up the pen, and wrote her vote.

Allie had already finished eating by the time she finally got the pen. She looked from face to face until she finally marked the paper and passed the pen back to its owner.

Drake dropped the pen on the table the second he touched it. "Oh gross! Who got syrup on this? It's my favorite pen!" Drake dipped his napkin in his water and used it to wipe down his writing utensil. Once he was confident he had dealt with the stickiness, he clipped it down the front of his T-shirt.

Ingrid and Allie looked at each other, then at Drake. "Sorry," they said in unison.

Everyone passed their votes to Drake, and he opened them up and showed them to the others as he did. It was a unanimous vote to go for the treasure.

"I have to admit, these results surprised me," Drake said. "I thought for sure you'd vote for something else, Allie."

"I almost did, but I figured we've come this far. Besides, it's been fun tromping all over town, trying to determine if we can solve the puzzle. It's certainly unlike any adventure that we've ever had before."

"That's for sure," Drake agreed.

"Now what's the second thing you wanted to discuss?" Allie asked.

Drake and Geneva looked at each other and back at Allie and Ingrid.

Geneva shifted in her chair and sat a little straighter. "Is there anything you two would like to share with the rest of the table?"

Allie's jaw dropped, and Ingrid blushed immediately, her cheeks turning a lovely pink.

"Like what?" Allie asked innocently.

"Oh, let's see. Like maybe an update in the relationship status on any social media apps?" Drake said.

"Okay, we give. What gave it away?" Allie asked.

"Um, perhaps the way you two look at each other gives us the entire story," Geneva said. "Also, there's the way you walk next to each other, close, but not too close, like you both have this desire to reach out for the other's hand but are too hesitant to do it."

Drake drained the last of his coffee and pointed at Allie. "And you weren't in your room all night. I doubt you spent the entire night up by the pool reading."

"How do you know I was gone?" Allie asked.

"The walls are paper thin. I can always tell when you're watching television, or listening to music while you're reading at night, but last night, it was stone quiet the entire time. Oh, and you left your room light on all night. I noticed it under the adjoining door every time I got up. Then this morning, the light went out, and the TV came on," Drake said.

"Okay, you got us, detective. We're busted," Ingrid said.

"So what?"

"So what?" Geneva asked. "So what?" she repeated, raising her voice. "So, congratulations. It took long enough for you two to get together. Geez, Allie, every time I see Ingrid, she talks about you, and it only takes a single look to understand that you two belong together."

Allie reached over and took Ingrid's hand. "I guess the jig is up. So now what?"

"Now we see about getting to that island," Drake said.

*

"You don't think they'll be mad at us since we took a minor detour, do you?" Allie asked.

Ingrid took her hands off the steering wheel just long enough to wave Allie's question away. "Of course not. We're only five minutes away from the marina. Besides, how long will it take us to look at a grave? Five, ten minutes at most? We'll just say we got held up at the market."

"I like where you're going with that. Someone paying with a check, holding up a really long line. Or maybe someone who used cash, with a ton of coins."

Ingrid grinned. "Exactly. Besides, we're already here." Ingrid pulled into a parking space in front of the church, threw Geneva's SUV into Park, and got out and joined Allie on the sidewalk. "You ready?"

Allie looked at the granite church, took a quick picture, then headed for the door. Once inside, the pair paid a donation to enter, then stepped into the building. Inside the church proper, the first stop was at box pew number fifty-four. There they found a simple brass plaque that read 'The Adams Pew', and the pew decorated with a red, white, and blue carnations, and a small American flag.

"What are you thinking?" Ingrid asked.

"Can you believe two presidents sat right here? I think that's amazing," Allie answered.

"Don't be amazed for too long. Remember. We're on the clock."

"Okay, you're right. Let's go downstairs."

Allie took a few pictures of the pew and the church's interior, then followed Ingrid to the steps to the crypt. Down below, Allie stopped and gazed at the graves of John Adams, John Quincy Adams, and their wives, Abigail and Louisa. She stared at the vaults for the longest time, lost in her thoughts about the American history that corresponded with only four people. She broke from her trance, took a few photos, and turned back to Ingrid.

"You know what we should do, you and me? We should go on a quest to visit the graves of every dead president."

"I thought maybe we might go to Paris or Rome, but okay, I suppose wandering around the country looking for dead people could be fun," Ingrid said.

Allie kissed Ingrid on the forehead. "I like your idea, too. I'm sure I could find plenty of famous graves to look at in Rome and Paris. There are probably plenty of geocaches to find there, too."

"But I'm not discounting your idea. We should rent an RV and make a really fun road trip out of it, right?"

Allie checked the time on her phone. "We need to get back to the marina. They're going to be waiting for us. I appreciate the side trip, though, sugar. Thanks for bringing me here."

Ingrid giggled.

"What?" Allie asked.

"You called me sugar."

The church was only ten minutes away from the marina, and for once, traffic worked for them rather than against them. Once they parked, Allie grabbed two bags of bottled sodas, and Ingrid retrieved a Styrofoam cooler from the back of the SUV and headed down the dock to the boat.

From the pier, Allie saw Drake and Geneva sitting in the

rear seats of the boat, not moving. "Hey, you two, mind giving us a hand down here?" Allie shouted from the dock.

Neither one responded, so Allie put her bags down and climbed aboard. "What's up? Didn't you hear me? Hello?"

Both Drake and Geneva looked at Allie but didn't speak.

"Please, join them," a voice said from behind her. Allie turned. Sitting on the deck, half-hidden by the console, was Stan. It took only a couple seconds to recognize he was holding a 9mm in his right hand. Allie's eyes darted from the gun to the deck between Stan and herself.

"No, don't think about it. There's no way you can cover that distance before I pull the trigger first. Please have your other friend come aboard and take a seat with the others," Stan said.

Allie put her hands out before her and turned toward the dock. "Ingrid. You want to come aboard, please?"

Ingrid stepped on the boat and set the cooler down next to the hull. "What's up?"

Allie cocked her head in Stan's direction, and Ingrid mimicked Allie's hands.

"Sit. I won't ask you again."

Although the rear seat could only comfortably seat three, Drake and Geneva squeezed in together to make room for Ingrid and Allie to sit down.

"What's the deal, Stan?" Allie asked. "What's this all about?"

Stan got to his feet and moved closer to the four. "The treasure, of course."

"You mean your book? Do you want it back?"

"No. You don't understand. Throughout the years, I've only sold a few dozen copies of that book. Although most go unread, now and then some ambitious people will take it upon themselves to track down the treasure. Of all of them, you four have gotten further along than anyone else ever."

"How could you possibly know that?" Drake asked. "How

did you even know to find us here?"

"The same way I've been tracking you ever since the cemetery. At first, I thought you were just normal tourists. But then your movements seemed a little too odd to be just seeing the sites. Especially the way you'd skip some of the most-visited tourist attractions, only to visit places not as well known."

"You didn't answer the question. How did you guess we were here?" Drake asked.

A sly smile crossed Stan's face. "There's a tracker in your book. Following you is as easy as looking at an app and reading a map."

"So then meeting you at the restaurant wasn't a coincidence?"

Stan shook his head. "Nope. In fact, I knew you would head there before you figured it out yourself. I was lucky enough to get there before you. I'm surprised you didn't see me in the next booth."

"And it was you I spotted following us that day," Allie said.

"Yes, it was. It was a good move for you to dip into that bookstore. I saw you, you know, peering around those books like you were playing hide and go seek. Although it hurts to admit it, I also must give you credit. It was smart for the four of you to go four different ways, but then again, I had the upper hand. I was following the book, regardless of who had it."

"So why make yourself known now?" Drake asked. He attempted to move a little to his right but couldn't.

"Because I saw you use the business center at the library, and it only took me a few keystrokes to figure out you were interested in an ocean voyage. The only problem is, you printed too much area for me to figure out where you were going to next, so I decided it was time to make myself known."

"We're just going out for a day on the water," Ingrid said.

Stan tipped his head back and expelled a hearty laugh. "I'm sure you are. I'm not quite the idiot you think I am."

"Fine. So then what's the plan, Stan?" Geneva asked.

Ingrid couldn't help herself and started giggling at the quip. Allie tried to hold back, but she laughed too.

Stan held the gun out and took a step forward. "You, you stop laughing at me! Now! I mean it."

Allie stopped right away and elbowed Ingrid in the ribs to stop her. Ingrid got the hint and contained herself.

"Seriously, what's next?" Drake asked.

"I figured I'd tag along on your little adventure. You wouldn't mind a third, would you?"

"Third? You mean fifth, don't you?" Geneva said.

Stan took a couple of steps back and leaned on the console. "No. I know how to count. I need to make sure I have some insurance out there, and that means splitting you up. Half of you will stay here. Half of you will go with me. If anyone steps out of line, I will assess penalties. You get me?"

"We get you. You expect us to play nice," Drake said. "If all goes as planned, how do you see this turning out?"

"Simple. We go out there and find the treasure, which you will turn over to me. Then we come back here, and I release all four of you. I get what I want, you get your freedom."

"What guarantee will you have that we won't go to the cops?" Geneva asked.

Stan rushed over and grabbed a handful of Geneva's hair, pulled her head forward, and pointed the gun at her temple. "Because I've discovered where you and the blond live. If any of you make the mistake of going to the police, one of you is going to have a deadly accident. You get me?"

Geneva whimpered, so Stan thrust her head back and went back to his position.

"Who stays and who goes?" Ingrid asked.

"We'll figure that out soon. In the meantime, you sit there and be quiet."

For the next twenty minutes, no one moved, and no one

spoke. Then, unexpectedly, Hailey appeared and stepped onto the boat, hoisting the bags that Allie had left on the dock.

"What's in here?" Hailey asked as she opened the bag and looked in. "Ugh. No beer? I suppose that's being a responsible boater. It would be a shame if some of you had too much to drink and fell overboard, right, Stan?"

"Yep, that's a fact."

"How are you sure the treasure is even out there?" Drake asked. "For all you know, it's but another step in the goose chase. There's no guarantee it's the end of the line, and nothing for sure says it even exists."

"Oh, I have my ways," Hailey said. "We've been chasing these ghosts for a long time. I always believed that it lies out there in the Atlantic somewhere, but we've never been able to figure out exactly where. That was the whole point of the book. To get people to do all the tough legwork for us, and from what Stan tells me, you're the closest anyone has ever come. Enough chat. Let's get this show on the road. Stan, who are you taking out to sea with you?"

Stan pointed in Drake's direction. "Him for sure. I don't care who else. You pick who stays."

Hailey approached the group and looked them over. Finally, her eyes settled on Allie. "You. Up."

When Allie didn't move, Hailey reached behind her and pulled a gun from the waistband of her pants and waved it in Allie's direction. "Perhaps you didn't understand me. I said up."

Allie slowly got to her feet, but when she didn't move fast enough, Hailey reached out for Allie's arm, and spun her toward the edge of the boat. Hailey stuck out her foot, tripped Allie, and Allie screamed as she flipped over the gunwale and landed face down on the dock. Ingrid made a move to jump up, but Hailey held out a hand and pushed her back into the seat. "You stay, you go."

Hailey pointed her gun at Geneva and motioned for her to

get up. Geneva looked at Drake for reassurance, and he nodded. "Go on. Take care of Allie. Everything will be okay."

Geneva moved quickly, left the boat, and dropped to Allie's side. Allie was grabbing her right knee and writhing in pain.

"Are you okay?" Geneva asked.

"Forget all that. Pick her up and let's go. Remember that I'm armed, and your friends will be in trouble if you don't comply," Hailey said as she stepped onto the dock.

Geneva crouched and helped Allie to her feet. Allie took a tentative step and almost fell again. Had Geneva not caught her, Allie would have fallen into the water.

"Come on, lean on me," Geneva said as she placed Allie's arm around her neck. Although it took a few minutes, Geneva struggled to get Allie to land. There was a bench nearby, and Geneva made for it and sat Allie down.

"Keep going," Hailey demanded.

"Come on, let her rest for a minute," Geneva pleaded.

"I said get up."

Geneva leaned over so Allie could put her arm around her again. "Hopefully it's not much farther, and you can sit down and rest."

"It's that white cargo van over there," Hailey said as she pointed to the parking area.

Geneva half-carried Allie to the van. Hailey opened the back doors, and Geneva and Allie got in. Hailey produced two pairs of handcuffs. She put one handcuff around Geneva's wrist and attached the other to a ring welded to the van wall and repeated the process with Allie.

Allie looked out the back door, hoping to see if she could get someone's attention. All she saw was the fishing boat carrying Drake and Ingrid leaving the harbor.

CHAPTER EIGHTEEN

As Drake drove the boat, he ran options through his mind about how to get out of the situation he was currently in. He checked the GPS on his phone to make sure he was still headed in the right direction and stole a glance behind him. Ingrid was sitting on the bench seat in the back, but Stan had handcuffed her to the gunwale. Their eyes met, and to Drake's surprise, he recognized anger and frustration behind her beautiful blues, but not fear. Stan was sitting on the far side of Ingrid, with his gun pointed at Drake's back.

Drake daydreamed about certain escape scenarios, but his ideas were limited to those he'd seen in the movies. He considered for a second, turning the engine to full throttle. Drake thought of steering violently from side to side, hoping to throw Stan overboard. Just as soon as he imagined it, he dismissed his plan because he didn't know how that would affect either himself or Ingrid. Likewise, he couldn't aim for the nearest patch of sand and beach the boat for the same reason. He believed Stan was more than capable of pulling the trigger, and expected that for now, he had to play the game straight.

"How long until we get to that island?" Stan yelled over the roar of the engines.

Drake didn't respond, so Stan stood, made his way to the captain's chair, and thrust his gun into Drake's side. Drake responded by pulling away, and when he did so, he jerked the wheel and almost fell. He feared he was going to dump the boat, so he eased the throttle back, switched into Neutral, straightened the wheel, and regained his footing.

Stan jabbed Drake in the side again. "What are you trying to pull?"

Drake bared his teeth and leered at Stan. "What do you mean? You snuck up on me. You're lucky I didn't tip this thing."

Stan stepped back. "I asked you a question. How long until we get to the island?"

"I have zero clue. Half an hour, maybe more. I'm not a sea captain. We'll get there when we get there."

"Go," Stan ordered.

Drake spun around and looked at Ingrid. She'd taken the worst of the jostling. She had tears streaming from her eyes, and she was rubbing her shoulder with her free hand. Drake left the wheel and rushed to her side.

"Are you okay?"

Ingrid shook her head. "When the boat lurched, I felt my shoulder pop."

"Okay, sit tight, okay. I'm going to look at it."

Drake reached for her, but Stan intervened. "Hey, get back to the wheel."

"Not until I check her out."

Stan considered pushing the issue and changed his mind. "Do it, but quick. We need to get back at it."

Drake turned his attention back to Ingrid and slowly inched his fingers along Ingrid's shoulder. She flinched at his touch and took a deep breath and tried to relax.

"It doesn't seem like you dislocated it. Probably pulled a

muscle, though. I'm sorry for my bad driving," Drake said. "Any chance you can lose the cuffs on her? She promises she'll be nice."

Drake stared at Stan, but Stan didn't move.

"Come on, where's she going to go? Jump overboard and swim back to shore?"

Stan didn't move.

Drake held his phone over the side of the boat. "Take off the cuffs or I drop my phone into the ocean and the coordinates to the treasure will go with it."

Stan considered it for a second and fished the handcuff keys from his pocket and tossed them to Drake. In a moment, Drake unlocked the cuff on Ingrid's wrist.

"Thanks," Ingrid said as she rubbed her wrist. "That was painful."

Drake smiled. "I'd suggest some ice and a couple aspirin, but I'm afraid we have neither. Can you hold on for a couple of hours? We'll be back to shore soon enough."

Ingrid gave him a tentative nod, and Drake moved back to the wheel. He rechecked his position, opened the throttle, and started out again. Ahead of him was nothing but open water, but eventually the land came into view. After a few more minutes, he throttled back.

"Why are you slowing down?" Stan asked.

Drake looked at the depth finder and watched as the numbers dropped. "I don't want to run aground anywhere. Unless you'd like to be stuck on a deserted island. I'll need to circle the island to discover if there's a place to go ashore. I really don't want to swim for it. "

"Just do what you need to do. Don't try anything funny, though. I've still got the gun."

Drake took it easy as they circled the island, and when they got to the far side, Drake spotted a jetty that extended out a hundred feet into the bay. Monitoring the water depth, Drake moved closer.

"Can you step off and take the line and find a place to tie up to?" Drake asked Stan.

"Yeah, right? I get off the boat so you can take off? Nice try. Let Blondie do it."

Drake turned and addressed Ingrid. "Do you think you can handle it?"

"I think so," Ingrid said.

"Can you at least toss her the bow line?" Drake asked.

"Okay. No quick moves from either of you. Got it?" Stan moved to the front and gathered the line while Ingrid opened the boarding door. She carefully stepped from the boat to the jetty, got her footing and caught the line that Stan threw to her.

"Where should I put this?" she asked.

Drake pointed to a spot a few feet to her left. "Wrap it around that part of the rock that's sticking up. I'll secure it better when I get there."

Once Ingrid secured the line, Drake cut the engine. Stan motioned with the gun for Drake to disembark, so Drake stepped over the side and joined Ingrid. He double checked the line, determined Ingrid had done a good enough job and waited while Stan got off the boat.

"Okay, move."

The rocks of the jetty were loose, so the three had to pick their way carefully to the shore.

"Now where to?" Stan asked once they got to the beach.

Drake shrugged. "I don't know. I guess we need to explore the island and see what we can see."

"That would take us all day," Stan said.

"I don't think so. It can't be any greater than two or three acres at most, and the vegetation isn't all that heavy. Seems to be mostly trees and small brush. It shouldn't take long to navigate around the entire island. Just pick a direction into the woods and go from there."

"Go then," Stan said.

Drake stood on the beach and looked at the tree line for a moment, picked out a spot to begin the search and started walking with Ingrid matching him step by step. Stan held back a few feet, then followed.

"Everything will be fine," Drake said.

"I hope so. I'm worried about Allie, though," Ingrid said. "She had a nasty fall, and I hope she's okay."

"Geneva will take good care of her. Allie is tough. She'll be good."

Ingrid looked over at Drake as she brushed her hair from eyes. "And what about us? Do you have a plan to get us out of this mess?"

"Honestly?" Drake asked.

"This would be a great time for it," Ingrid said.

"No. I don't have one. Do you?"

Ingrid picked up her pace by a half step. "Get in front of me and enter those the trees over to your right where that sapling is. Once we get into the trees, I'll give the signal, and we'll run. You go left, I'll go right, and I'll meet you back at the boat."

"Wait, no, what are you planning to do?"

Ingrid didn't answer, but Drake did as she asked and passed into the trees. When Ingrid passed by the sapling, she grabbed hold of the branch and bent it forward as she walked. When she estimated Stan had entered, she let go of the sapling. It snapped back and caught Stan right in the face.

"Drake, run!" Ingrid yelled.

Drake took off like a rabbit. He'd taken only three steps at most when he heard a gunshot ring out and he stopped dead in his tracks.

"Ingrid? Ingrid? Answer me!" Drake screamed.

Drake turned around and jogged back to where he'd entered the woods. When he returned to the scene, he saw Ingrid lying on the ground on her side. He rushed to her and dropped to his knees. "Ingrid? Hey? Can you hear me?"

He gently rolled her onto her back, felt the warm wetness, and saw the blood on her hand.

"Oh no, Ingrid," Drake said.

"She got what she deserved for pulling a stunt like that," Stan said.

Drake looked over and spotted Stan on his butt. Stan had the gun still extended, and whether Drake actually saw the smoking muzzle, or if that part was all in his imagination, he didn't know.

Drake's muscles tensed, and he wanted to rush the man, but held off when Stan raised the gun.

"She was an accident. You won't be," Stan muttered, a tinge of boredom in his tone.

Drake hesitated and turned his attention back to Ingrid. He lifted her T-shirt and winced at the blood coming from her side. Another inch, and the bullet would have missed her completely.

"This is going to hurt. I'm sorry." Drake rolled Ingrid to him and checked her other side, noticed no exit wound, and gently placed her back down. In response, Ingrid moaned.

"Can I go get a first aid kit from the boat?" Drake asked.

Stan got back to his feet but kept his distance. "You know the answer to that. Come on. It's time to go."

"Wait. Give me a minute." Drake took off his T-shirt, folded it in quarters and pressed it to Ingrid's wound. "Ingrid? Can you hear me? Ingrid?"

Ingrid moaned and her eyes fluttered open. "Drake? What happened?" Her voice was barely over a whisper, and Drake had to lean close to her mouth to hear her.

"You got shot. You'll be okay, but I need to leave you for a few minutes. Can you hold this tight?" Drake took Ingrid's hand and placed it on top of his shirt, but her hand dropped away immediately. He scanned the ground and found a large, flat rock a foot in diameter. "Lay still," he said.

Drake placed the rock on top of the T-shirt. He watched it

for a moment and thought it would tip off. Drake stacked more rocks next to Ingrid's side to give the rock's weight something else to lean against without falling.

"Let's go," Stan said.

Drake leaned in close to Ingrid. "I'll be back for you. I promise. We'll get out of this."

Drake got to his feet and wiped his bloody hands on his jeans, then walked into the woods with Stan.

"What are we looking for?" Stan asked.

"I don't know. Anything that looks man-made would be a good start. Of course, since we're looking for something from the 1700s, it might only be a pile of rocks by now."

Drake walked forward through the trees, and as he did, he scanned to the left and right. He searched for anything around other than natural rocks, trees, and bushes, but he noticed nothing else as he went. After a hundred yards, he stepped out of the tree line and found himself on the rocky beach on the opposite side of the island.

"Left, or right?" Drake asked aloud, mostly to himself.

"I'd go right," Stan said, answering the rhetorical question.

Out of spite, Drake turned left and started walking along the shoreline. A gull pierced the silence, and on instinct, Drake looked out at the water until he spotted the bird. He stopped for a moment and closed his eyes. Despite his current situation, it was a nice day. Blue sky, warm sun, nice and quiet. The way he liked it.

"What are you doing? Keep moving," Stan said.

"I was only reflecting on what a great day it is. Weather-wise, at least. Of course, being kidnapped and having my friend shot has put a damper on it pretty quick. I don't know what you're expecting to find out here, and you will not get away with shooting Ingrid."

"I will if I shoot you, too. Then you can die out here with her, and I take the boat back, and no one will ever be the wiser."

"You can't shoot me. You need me to find your treasure. Imagine the book sales you'll make when you do a second edition and explain how you found it."

Stan scratched his temple with the gun barrel. "Thanks for the idea. I hadn't even thought about that. It would be an excellent ending to the book."

"Yeah, but you'll have to keep me alive to tell you how we got this far."

"You're wrong about that. I only need to keep one of you alive. Or did you forget I have two others back on shore that I'm sure I could get the information out of, especially when you and the blond don't return?"

Drake scanned the beach and considered finding a rock large enough to hit Stan with. Deep inside, he understood he didn't have the reflexes to do it without getting shot, and if he was going to keep his promise to Ingrid, he needed to keep his head.

"What's that up there?" Stan asked.

"Huh?" Drake snapped out of his reverie and spotted the structure Stan was referring to. "Beats me. Let's go see."

As they approached, Drake saw it was the foundation of a long-destroyed building. Whatever was there before was just a pile of rubble in the center surrounded by walls that were part brick, part island stone. He walked around the remains and determined it had been eight feet square, and the walls that surrounded it ranged in height from four feet to nothing.

"Is this what you want?" Stan asked.

"Hard to say. It's not like there's a certificate of authenticity with the date of creation stuffed under a rock. The best we can do is check out the site and see if there's anything to tell us how long it's been here."

Stan sat on a portion of the wall and pointed his gun at Drake. "You best get at it, then. Remember, you're on the clock. I don't know how long the blond will last with the bullet in her belly."

Drake started at a corner and duck-walked his way along the wall, looking for any indications of what it was and when whoever made it. It wasn't until he got to the third corner that he found a brick that captured his attention. He tried to move it with his hands, and although it shifted, it didn't come free from the structure. He found a small, sharp-edged rock to use as a chisel, and another to use as a hammer, then went to work chipping away the stones from around the brick.

For ten minutes, he tried to free the brick, then finally, with a great yank, he freed it from the stone. Written on the side of the brick were the words 'Boston 1775', and when he turned it over, a small silver snuffbox slid away from the hollowed-out brick.

He opened the box, and inside was a small piece of an animal hide and written on the hide were words he couldn't make out in the shade under which he'd been working. Drake closed the snuff box and shoved it into his pocket, and put the hide inside the brick, and clambered to his feet.

"I've got something here," Drake said as he held up the brick.

Stan stood. "Toss it over."

Drake threw the brick toward Stan, and although he thought Stan was going to catch it, he let it drop, and the brick broke in half when it hit the ground. Stan saw the hide, bent over, and picked it up.

"What does it say?" he said as he examined the writing.

"I'm not sure. I couldn't make it out."

Stan threw the hide back at Drake. "It would be in your best interest to figure it out."

Drake caught the hide and stepped into the sunlight. Even then, he couldn't make out the words. He touched the writing, and noticed although the ink was age-worn, the depressions from whatever tool etched the words were still sharp.

Drake thought for a moment, then walked past Stan and

halted at the edge of the woods. He stopped in front of a bush that had a crop of bright red berries growing on it. Drake tucked the hide into his back pocket, then started picking berries from the bush, and when he had a good handful, he carried them to the water's edge. He found a flat stone large enough to hold the three-inch by two-inch piece of hide. He put the hide on the rock then covered it completely with the berries. Drake folded the hide in half, simulating a berry sandwich, then placed another rock on top of the hide. He pressed as hard as he could, grinding the top rock down into the hide. He took off the top rock, unfolded the hide, brushed away the smash berry residue, and gave the hide a quick rinse in the water.

Drake held up the hide and looked at it again. Although he had erased the remaining writing on the hide, the berry juice had leeched perfectly into the depressions. The writing looked as if someone had written it in a red pen only a few moments before.

"Did that work? What does it say?" Stan asked.

"The script is still hard to make out, but I believe it says two-hundred paces into the sun, then into the maw three man's lengths."

"What does that mean?"

"I'm pretty sure it means we found another clue to find the treasure. Hopefully, this one will lead to the treasure itself and we can be done with this."

"It better, for your sake," Stan said.

CHAPTER NINETEEN

"Two hundred paces into the sun." Drake looked up at the sky, but the sun was almost directly overhead. He dug his phone out of his pocket, opened a compass app, and determined where the east was.

Stan noticed Drake was using his phone, so he moved forward like a snake's strike and pulled Drake's phone from his hand.

"Texting for help, are you?"

"No. That's not the case at all. I'm trying to locate the next spot. I needed to determine where the directions were sending us."

Stan raised his gun and pointed the firearm at Drake's head. "I told you no games."

Drake put his hands out in front of him. "It's not a game. There's a way we can find the place without wandering blindly all over the island."

"How?"

"There's an app for that. Look, I'm a geocacher. I have an app on my phone that can project a waypoint. You don't even have to give me the phone back. You can do it."

"How?"

"Open up the phone. If the lock screen is on, the code is zero three one six. On the main screen, there's an app called 'Tools'. Go into that. All you need to do is enter the starting coordinates, angle, and distance, and it will calculate the coordinates of where we need to go."

Stan unlocked the screen, found the app, but couldn't figure it out. Instead, he passed the phone back to Drake. "You do it. But I'm going to watch. No funny stuff."

"Right. No funny stuff. Follow me."

Drake returned to the corner of the building where he'd found the brick and held the phone so Stan could watch his every move. He opened the app, selected an option to use his current coordinates, and entered ninety as the angle to represent an eastern heading. "How long do you suppose a pace is?"

Drake looked at Stan for an answer, but Stan didn't know.

"Let's assume a yard. Three feet. Three times two is six, so I'll enter six hundred for the distance." Drake waited for the microsecond it took for the app to do the calculations. When he looked at the screen again, he noticed not only the projected coordinates, but a line to guide him to the location.

"That's where we need to be. Almost to the far end of the island. We need to hurry, though."

"Why?" Stan asked.

"I'm down to four percent charge on my phone. It's going to die soon." Drake winced at the poor choice of words he'd selected. "Come on."

Drake glanced at the app to estimate the general area of the projected location, then started swiftly walking along the shoreline.

"Hey," Stan yelled, "this isn't due east. Where are you going?"

Drake pointed up at the shoreline. "We'll walk along the

beach for a few hundred feet and cut over into the trees. It'll save us time and effort without having to pick our way around bushes and whatnot."

They walked four hundred feet up the beach. When he noticed the shore was going to curl around in the opposite direction from where they needed to go, Drake stopped. He got his bearings and pointed into the trees. "We need to head that way. It looks like there's a hill to go up, but it doesn't seem too bad from here."

Drake looked at his battery percentage, and as he did, the number dropped from four to three. He selected a bent over tree fifty feet in the distance as a waymark and headed toward it, paying close attention to his footing as he did. Once he got to the tree, he picked another unique tree and picked his way through the underbrush until he reached it.

Drake checked his app and adjusted his position, so he was facing the direction he needed to go. He realized his battery had dropped to two percent, so he shut it off, hoping he would have enough power to make one phone call for help if he got the chance.

"We need to hike up this little mound," Drake said to Stan. The mound was more of a hill, and a steep one at that as it rose to an apex thirty feet above their heads. Unlike the rolling hills Drake climbed in the area around Nashville, the one before him was primarily rock. There was an intermittent tree or bush that had taken root over time, and Drake eyed their positions for use as potential handholds.

"I'm glad Allie's not here," Drake whispered to himself as the hill reminded him of the one Allie had injured herself on the previous year.

Drake leaned over, and using his hands and his feet, he began his ascent. Remembering Allie's tumble, Drake was careful to make sure that he planted each foot securely before he put weight on it and pushed his way up. The climb up the hill took him eleven minutes, and when he finally arrived at the top, it surprised him to find a large tree a few feet to his left. He walked to the tree and sat down in its shade.

As he waited for Stan to appear, he looked around. The hilltop was crescent-shaped and was forty-five feet at its widest point. He viewed the ocean and two other landmasses, although he didn't know what they were. Drake got back to his feet and looked over the side to check on Stan, hoping he'd fallen down the hill, but he was slowly but surely making progress toward him.

Drake figured he had another couple of minutes, so he hustled to the end of the point and looked out into the distance. From where he was, he barely made out the boat's stern in the distance. He figured it was maybe a quarter of a mile away.

"What are you doing?" Stan shouted.

Drake turned around and noticed Stan getting his second foot up and beneath him.

"Checking the view while waiting for you."

"Fine. I'm here. So now what?"

"The thing said into the maw, so look around for a maw, a hole, or something," Drake said.

Drake held back and watched as Stan walked back and forth across the hilltop. As Stan looked away, Drake glanced down the hill from where he stood. He thought about making his escape from there. When he took a better look, he acknowledged the ten-foot vertical drop to solid stone, so he knew he couldn't go that way. He followed the perimeter and hoped for an area he could scramble down in a hurry, but based on what he saw, the best way down was the way they'd come up.

"Hey, over here," Stan yelled.

Drake glanced in Stan's direction and saw him standing next to a depression in the stone, and as Drake approached, he saw that the depression opened into a hole.

"Here's your maw," Stan said as he pointed to the hole. "Go

check what's in that."

Drake looked at the hole and groaned. It was a rough oval with the center about four feet wide, and he could tell from where he stood it dropped three feet and slanted away into the darkness.

"Go."

"There's no way. I'm not going into that thing," Drake objected.

Stan rolled his eyes, racked the slide of his gun, aimed it close to Drake's feet, and pulled the trigger. The report was loud and there was an audible ricochet off the rock, and Drake jumped back a foot out of instinct.

"Oops," Stan said. "Accident. If you don't want me to have another accident, one that ends up in your chest, I suggest you get in that hole."

Drake stared into Stan's eyes, then when Stan racked the slide again, Drake turned his attention to the hole. He got down on his knees, dropped his head into the gap, and prayed there was nothing in there that didn't like company.

"It's too dark in there. I can't see anything after, like, three feet. We'll have to go back to the boat and check if there's a flashlight aboard."

"Nope. No way," Stan said. "Use the light on your phone."

Drake shook his head. "Sorry, man, no can do. My battery is dead like a doornail. The only way I'm getting light from my phone is if I set it on fire."

"Use mine then," Stan said as he produced his phone. He unlocked the screen and turned on the light, then relocked the screen before he handed it over to Drake.

Drake took the phone, hung his legs over the hole, and dropped in. He shined the light forward and saw that the sides and ceiling had grooves, like tool marks, in them. Drake also sensed that the tunnel slanted forward for about four feet before it ended. The tunnel was spacious enough for him to duck walk to the end, and when he got there, he found the tunnel didn't end abruptly, but ended in another hole.

Drake shined the light into the hole and saw a small cavern ten feet below him. He thought about turning around and going to get some rope when the light caught a reflection on the wall below him. He leaned into the void and reached the phone out as far as he dared. The light was enough for him to see that there were iron bars embedded in the walls, starting three feet below him and ending a foot or two above the floor.

Drake turned around, got on his belly, and inched backward until his legs dropped over the edge. He flailed his feet until one of them connected with the iron rod, and he put his foot on top of it. Without fully committing, he tested to see if the rung would hold his weight, and when he trusted it would, he went for it and stood. The rod held, so holding on to the tunnel floor for support, he dropped and found the next rung on which to put his other foot. Slowly, he stepped from rung to rung until, finally, his feet hit the stone floor of the cavern.

Once in the cavern, Drake took a better look around. The cavern was almost a perfect circle, and the floor sloped downward to the center of the circle. Drake followed the slope and in the center of the room he found nine holes, each an inch in diameter, drilled into the floor. The floor was completely empty, save for a pile of brown leaves and small sticks near the holes. He left the center and stepped to a wall at random and followed the arc of the circle. Halfway around the circle, he found an area where the arc jutted out slightly from the rest of the wall, overlapping itself. Where the arc stopped was an enormous pile of stones and rubble that stood almost all the way to the ceiling. Drake thought he was at a dead end and was going to leave when he spotted a sideways brick in the stone pile. He cleared away enough rocks to free the brick, and using the light, he saw an imprint of Boston 1775, just like the other he found.

He set the brick aside and got to work clearing away the

stones, and after twenty minutes, he'd removed enough to see the debris was concealing a small hallway. Once he opened a hole big enough to pass through, he moved forward, having to shuffle sideways to do so. After twenty feet, the hallway opened into another room.

The room was only twenty-five feet square and six feet high, and bricks, not stone, made up the walls. Each brick had a marking from being made in Boston. He pushed on the wall closest to him, hoping to find a secret door, but the wall was firm. Drake moved to the wall opposite, and pushed on that one, too, but again, nothing budged. He eyed one brick that looked unlike the others, since it had a marking of 'Boston 1775'.

Drake tapped on the brick and found it made a distinct sound from its neighbor. He slid back into the passageway far enough to find a baseball-sized rock, then headed back into the room. Drake located the brick again, then smashed the rock against it. It took three hits before the brick gave way and fell to the floor. Behind where the brick had been Drake discovered a depression. Drake used the phone's flashlight to peek inside, and he saw another piece of hide.

He removed the hide from the hole, unwrapped it, and found a large iron key. He wrapped the key back in the hide, then examined the remaining bricks. On the back wall, Drake discovered four other bricks that weren't like the others and used the rock to break them. Behind each of the broken bricks, he found an indentation, and within the indentation, he found an iron bar. He reached in, pulled on the bar, and a corner of the facade broke away from the wall. Once he pulled all the bars, the bottom part of the wall fell away.

Once the dust settled, Drake looked where the wall had been and found a large wooden chest. He struggled to pull the chest out of the wall and into the room, but with extra effort, he managed the task. Drake found the chest locked but based on the size of the lock hole in the front, Drake guessed he already had the key.

Drake extracted the key from his pocket, slid it into the keyhole, and turned it. At first it wouldn't go, but after a couple minutes of wiggling it back and forth, the key finally turned all the way, and the lock popped open. Drake opened the chest, took a deep breath, and looked inside.

The only item in the chest was a silver snuffbox, a duplicate of the one he had in his pocket. He removed the box from the chest and opened it. Inside the cover were a few engraved words, and inside the box was a silver key, the size of a modern house key. Drake closed the snuffbox and put it in his back pocket, then he removed the key from the chest lock, wrapped it back up in the hide, and stowed that in his front pocket.

He left the room, backtracked to the cavern, and used the iron bars to climb up to the main tunnel. Soon after, he sensed daylight, crawled to the entrance, and poked his head up into the fresh air.

"You've been gone long enough," Stan said. "What did you find?"

"It's down there. The treasure. Loads of it," Drake said.

Stan looked at him, disbelieving.

Drake pulled the snuffbox from his front pocket. "For real. Here. I brought this back." Drake held the box out and Stan greedily grabbed it.

Stan examined the box, then put it in his pocket. "That's it? Silver?"

Drake shook his head. "No. There's silver and gold. Lots of gold. I only brought that up because it was easy for me to carry."

"Get back in there, then. Show me where it is. I'll follow you."

"No, you can't. There's not enough room. Whoever built this place made sure it would only handle one person at a time. You got it though, all the treasure. All you need to do is go down there and get it."

Drake got out of the hole and took a few steps away to the edge of the hill. Stan took the box from his pocket and marveled at how it reflected the sun.

"Thanks for the help," Stan said. He lifted the gun, and without really aiming, fired a bullet in Drake's direction.

Drake fell over the hill and disappeared. Stan walked over to the edge and looked at Drake's prone, unmoving body, then went back to the hole and entered the way Drake had done.

While hiking in the woods, Drake once came across an opossum. When the possum spotted him, the animal rolled over and played dead, and that was the exact thing Drake was doing. The bullet had come close enough to his face for him to hear the buzz as it passed, and he threw himself over the edge. Although he didn't fall far, landing on the rocks was enough to knock the breath out of his lungs. He wanted to cry out, but he bit his lip and stayed as still as he could, hoping that Stan wouldn't pepper his body with more shots. If he did, Drake knew he was dead for sure.

He felt Stan's shadow fall over him. It hesitated for a few seconds, then Drake felt the warmth of the sun on his back again. Drake waited and slowly counted to ninety, then slowly turned his head and moved slightly so he could glance up the hill. Stan wasn't there, so Drake noiselessly got to his feet and climbed down the hill as silently as he could.

When he got to the bottom, he looked up at the hill to the spot where the point of the crescent was to give him an idea of the boat's direction. He started running as fast as he could through the woods, which wasn't faster than a slow jog. As he ran, the bush and tree branches slapped against his legs and his bare chest, and twice he fell when he wasn't paying attention to his footing. Finally, he broke through the trees and spotted the boat only fifty feet away.

Drake ran toward the boat, then changed direction and made for the spot where he'd left Ingrid. He dropped to his knees, and at first glance, noticed Ingrid hadn't moved a centimeter since he'd left her side.

"Ingrid? Can you hear me?" Drake reached for her neck and exhaled when he found a pulse. It was weak, but it was there. Drake removed the rock from Ingrid's belly and lifted his shirt. When he did, the wound oozed a little, but Drake knew it was time to go. He pushed the shirt back over the wound.

"I'm going to lift you up now."

As gently as he could, Drake lifted Ingrid from the ground and carried her to the jetty. He hesitated for a moment, picked his path with his eyes, then started slowly walking over the uneven rocks to the boat. Once there, he laid Ingrid across the back seat, jumped back onto the jetty to untie the bow line, then got back on the boat. Drake started the engine, reversed away from the island, then put it into gear and pointed the bow toward the mainland.

CHAPTER TWENTY

When he was a few hundred yards away from the island, Drake put the boat in Neutral and checked all the compartments of the boat until he found the first aid kit. From that, he dressed Ingrid's wound with something more than just a dirty T-shirt.

"Ingrid? Are you still with me?" Drake asked as he checked her pulse again. He shook his head and realized he had to get her medical attention as quickly as he could.

Drake pushed the engine as fast as he dared, fearful that the boat bouncing over the waves would throw Ingrid off the seats and onto the deck. As he steered back toward the marina, he tried to use the marine radio to call for help, but since he had never used one before, he quickly gave it up out of frustration.

Drake finally spotted the marina and made for it, and when he felt he was close enough, he pulled his phone from his pocket. The cracked screen made him worry he'd broken it, but when he pressed the power button, the phone came to life. He looked at the battery percentage and grew immediately concerned that he had enough life left in it for only one call. With one hand on the wheel, he called for help.

As Drake came into the marina, he spotted Hailey waiting for them on the dock. When he got close enough to drift, Drake killed the engine. A few seconds later, the boat jarred when it came into contact with the old car tires that acted as bumpers on the dock. He threw the bowline to Hailey, and while she tied off the bow, he opened the side door, left the boat, and tied off the stern line.

"Where's Stan?" Hailey asked as Drake rushed to step back on the boat.

"Where are my friends?" Drake asked in return.

"Where's Stan?" Hailey pulled the gun from her waistband and pointed it at Drake.

Drake stopped and raised his hands in the air. "He's back on the island waiting for you. We found the treasure."

He wondered for a moment if he should rush Hailey, rip the gun from her hands, and give her the same treatment Ingrid had received.

"Why did he send you back?" Hailey asked.

"Stan shot my friend, and as a sign of appreciation, he sent me back with her. He wants you to come back with the boat. All I want is an ambulance. Y'all can have the boat and the treasure. It means nothing to us."

Hailey looked over the edge of the boat and glanced at Ingrid's prone body in the back seat, but she seemed skeptical and wasn't buying a word of it. "Why didn't he call me? He said he would call if he found something."

"The treasure's hidden underground in a cavern. Surrounded by stone. Couldn't make a call from there."

"I think you're lying," she said, point blank.

"No, wait, I can show you." Drake dug into his pocket and removed the hide. He uncovered the key and showed it to Hailey. "He sent me back with this as proof. This is the key that opened a giant chest filled with gold and silver. Let me get my friend medical attention. You take the boat, and that will be the end.

We'll go our separate ways from here."

Off in the distance, sirens pierced the mid-afternoon peace.

"Your time is running out, Hailey. That's the police and, hopefully, an ambulance. I called them when we got close to the shore. You still have time to get on the boat and get out of here. Tell me where my friends are and take the boat. For both of our sakes."

Hailey looked in Drake's eyes, then out toward the parking lot, then back at Drake. "Get your friend off my boat."

Drake dropped his arms, then jumped back on the boat. He picked up Ingrid. She moaned but had the strength to put an arm around his neck. By the time Drake stepped off the boat, Hailey was there holding the bow and stern lines and when Drake cleared the door, Hailey got on the boat and closed the door.

"Your friends are in the white van. Keys are in the ignition." Hailey started the engine, shifted into Reverse, and pulled away from the dock.

Drake carried Ingrid to the end of the pier and into the parking lot. Just as he got to the van, two squad cars tore into the lot and stopped in a V-shape behind the van.

The officers erupted from each car and pointed their guns at Drake. "Put down the girl!" one of them screamed at Drake.

Drake complied, kneeled, and placed Ingrid gently on the ground, then dropped to his knees and put his hands behind his head. "I'm the one who called you. There's one getting away on a boat, the one who shot her is on an island out in the bay. I have two more friends locked in this van here. The keys are in it."

While one officer held a gun on Drake, the other placed him in handcuffs, took him away from Ingrid's side, and leaned him over the hood of his squad car. Once Drake was in custody, the other officer called for an ambulance, then crept to the back door of the van and, gun drawn, threw it open. He put his gun back in his holster, unlocked the women from their handcuffs, and helped them out of the van.

Allie saw Ingrid laying on the ground and made a move toward her, but when she put weight on her right leg, she screamed, lost her balance, and fell to the ground.

Geneva watched Allie lying on the ground, writhing in pain as she clutched her knee. She knew she had a decision to make, and neither choice was the correct one. She chose the unconscious friend, ran to Ingrid, dropped to her knees, and put her hands on Ingrid's face. "Ingrid! Ingrid? Drake, what happened to her?"

"Stan shot her," Drake yelled.

Geneva glanced at Drake, handcuffed and sitting on the pavement, his back to the squad car's front tire.

Geneva looked back down at her friend and took Ingrid's hand. "You'll be okay. Help will be here soon. Hang on."

A few seconds later, an ambulance pulled into the parking lot. The EMTs got out and immediately attended to Ingrid, determined she was stable enough for transport, got her on a gurney, and placed her into the ambulance. Once Ingrid was secure, the EMTs came back for Allie and attended to her as well. Within five minutes, two out of four of the friends were on their way to the hospital.

Geneva stepped over to Drake and told the officer holding him about everything that had happened that day. Eventually, the trooper removed the handcuffs from Drake. It took an hour between the two of them to give a statement to the police and have it validated. Finally, the police put a BOLO out on Stan and Hailey, and Drake and Geneva retreated to the SUV.

Once they were alone, they embraced, each not wanting to let the other go.

"Well, now what?" Geneva asked. "Should we go to the hospital?"

Drake shook his head. "I don't think we have time. Don't you have a concert tonight that you can't miss?"

Geneva checked the clock in the car. "Yes, you're right. I'd forgotten it was Friday today. I don't need to be there for another three hours."

"It might take that long to get Ingrid through surgery, and for Allie to get looked at. We wouldn't be able to visit them before then."

"So, what do you propose?"

"Let's take a quick ride out to Lexington."

"Lexington? Why do you want to go there?"

Drake reached around and took the snuffbox from his back pocket, opened it up, and handed it to Geneva. She took it and looked inside. "Oh, my." She passed the box back to Drake and put the car in gear.

Forty-five minutes later, Geneva pulled her car into an old Lexington cemetery. She followed the road until they found the mausoleum they were looking for. They got out of the car, and as they walked to the entrance, Drake removed the key from the box.

"You don't think this is really going to work, do you?" Geneva asked as Drake put the key in the lock.

Drake attempted to turn the key, but it didn't budge. "I guess not." Dejected, Drake climbed down the three steps and sat down.

Geneva sat by his side and took his hand. "Well, we've had a good run. It's time to give it up. There's been enough blood, sweat, and tears shed over this adventure."

"Yeah. I feel bad for Ingrid. And for Allie. I hope they're going to be okay."

Drake had barely finished the sentence when Geneva's phone rang. She looked at the screen, then took the call. Once it connected, she fumbled with the buttons until she activated the speaker.

"Hello? Are you there?" Allie said from the box.

"Allie? How are you doing?" Drake asked.

"I'm okay. They gave me something for the pain. I'm waiting for X-rays and to see a doctor. I'll probably be here a few hours yet."

"What about Ingrid?" Geneva asked.

"That's why I'm calling. She woke up in the ambulance and told me to give you a message. It's Friday, don't forget about your concert. Then she passed out again."

"Is she okay?" Drake asked.

"I don't know. The last update I got was she was going into surgery, and that was forever ago. I have to go. I'll call back later."

Without saying goodbye, Allie ended the call, leaving Geneva staring at her phone.

"Come on, let's go. We should probably head for the show." Geneva got to her feet and tugged Drake's arm. As he got up, he took one last look at the mausoleum, then took three steps toward the car, and stopped.

"What is it?" Geneva asked.

Drake went back to the mausoleum and kneeled. He ran his fingers along a brick. "Boston, 1775."

"Yeah, so?"

"You wouldn't have a hammer and a chisel in your SUV, would you?"

"No chisel. But I probably have a hammer and a screwdriver in the toolbox in the trunk. Would that do?"

Drake smiled.

Fifteen minutes later, Drake freed the brick from the mausoleum. He turned it over, and a key slid out of the hollow brick. He placed the brick back in the wall, then returned to the mausoleum door. He put the key in the lock, turned it, and unlocked the door.

Inside the mausoleum were two six-sided oak coffins, each one with a silver lock on the front. Geneva took the silver key Drake had given her. She slipped the key into the lock and hesitated.

"I hope there's not a squishy body in here," she said.

"If there is someone in there, they'd just be bones by now. You want to go outside while I do this?" Drake asked.

"No," Geneva said. "I'm good."

Geneva turned the key, unlocked the lock, and together, Geneva and Drake opened the coffin.

Geneva had her eyes closed, and when she opened them, she didn't see a body at all. Instead, she saw several leather pouches. Drake pulled the top one from the pile and carefully opened it. He pulled out the first document and set it on the pouch. Silently, they both read the document for a few moments.

"Holy cow. Is that a letter from George Washington?" Geneva asked.

"Yeah, I believe it is. Allie's going to freak when she sees this."

"Are these bags all filled with correspondence?"

Drake shrugged. "Your guess is as good as mine. The only way to find out is to go through them all."

Drake opened each of the pouches enough to glance inside to see what they contained. Every pouch held documents.

"I don't think we should disturb these. I wouldn't want to destroy anything," Geneva said.

"Yeah, I agree. We need to turn this over to a museum or something."

"What's in the other coffin?" Geneva asked.

"I don't know. The squishy body you're hoping for?" Drake teased.

Geneva took the key from the coffin and unlocked the other one. When they lifted the lid, they discovered more pouches, but instead of being filled with documents, they found gold, silver, and precious stones.

"Oh, my," Geneva said. "I think we're rich."

"Well, someone is for sure," Drake said. "I'm fairly certain once we call this in, it won't be a case of finders, keepers. I can only imagine that the cemetery or the city will claim ownership."

"You're probably right. Still, we have to call someone about all this, right?"

Drake rubbed his chin. "Yes. This is a treasure that we should share with the country. But not today. We've got a concert to go to. Let's put everything back together and head out."

* * *

"Hey, you," Ingrid said softly.

Allie looked up from the book she was reading. She smiled when she saw Ingrid looking at her, then put the book down and picked her crutches up. Allie maneuvered to Ingrid's bedside and took Ingrid's hand. "Hey yourself. How are you feeling?"

"I'm exhausted. What time is it?"

"It's three in the afternoon on Sunday."

The information confused Ingrid. "Sunday? What happened?"

Allie sat on the bed awkwardly, unable to get her full-leg brace into a suitable position. "You got shot, remember? Drake brought you back. You didn't lose any organs, but you lost a lot of blood. I was so scared when I first saw you. You were so pale."

"I'm a Dane," Ingrid joked weakly.

"You were paler than a Dane should be. They got the bullet out without any problems. You're still getting intravenous fluids and antibiotics. You'll be fine though and should be out of here in a couple of days."

"Do I have a big scar?"

"I don't know. I haven't seen it. It's okay, though. I think scars are sexy."

"Can I have some water?"

Allie got off the bed, found the bed's controls, raised the head of the bed, and pressed the call button. When the nurse answered, Allie requested water for her friend.

"What's up with your leg?" Ingrid asked.

"I whacked it pretty good when I got thrown off the boat. Lucky for me, it's just another terrible sprain, and I won't require surgery, but I won't be out skiing or mountain climbing for a long time."

A nurse entered the room carrying a Styrofoam cup. "Good to see you awake, Ingrid. Do you mind if I check your vitals while I'm here?"

"Go ahead," Ingrid said.

As the nurse gave Ingrid a once-over, Allie stepped back to the chair and sat down. The nurse checked Ingrid's pulse, temperature, respiration, and blood pressure. Afterwards, she checked the fluid levels Ingrid was getting.

"All is good here," the nurse said. She handed Ingrid the cup. "Here are some ice chips for you. Once you get through these, we'll see if we can get you something fancy, like Jell-O or some broth."

"Ooh," Ingrid said, "I can't wait. I hope it's orange."

The nurse smiled, patted Ingrid on the shoulder, then left the room.

"Where are Geneva and Drake? Are they okay?" Ingrid asked.

"Yeah, they're fine. They're busy cleaning out a crypt." Allie said.

"What?"

"On the island, Drake found a key, and the key led to a cemetery mausoleum. Inside two coffins, they found papers and gold and other stuff dating back to the revolution."

"Wouldn't that all belong to the cemetery?"

"You'd think so, but when they built the mausoleum, the builders wrote a five-hundred-year contract with the cemetery. It stated whoever had the key was the rightful owner of whatever was held within. Drake found that key, which made him the owner." Allie explained.

"That sounds really suspect," Ingrid said.

"I agree. I imagine it's all going to end up in court at some point, but Geneva, Drake, and I all agree that we need to donate most of the stuff to a museum, anyway. If we're lucky, we'll get a nice finder's fee out of it."

Ingrid spooned an ice chip out of the cup and chomped on it. "What happened to Stan and Hailey? Did they get caught?"

"Oh yeah. I almost forgot about them. The story's been all over the news. The Coast Guard picked Hailey up. She didn't know where the island exactly was, so she just did laps in the Atlantic until she eventually ran out of gas. What an idiot. They found Stan in the dark in a cave on the island. I heard when they finally found him, he was crying like a baby. Either way, she's facing charges for kidnapping and theft of the boat, and he's on the hook for kidnapping and attempted murder."

Allie's phone buzzed, so she picked it up to check the message. "Your parents will be back soon. They went out to get a bite to eat."

"My parents are here?"

"Yep. They came in yesterday, remember?"

Ingrid shook her head.

"Yeah, I didn't think so. You were pretty out of it. I really like them. They've been telling me stories about you."

"Oh, no," Ingrid moaned.

"Don't worry. Nothing too embarrassing. I asked them to save that stuff until you were back with us so I could watch your expression as they talked."

"That's evil," Ingrid said.

"I know. I learned it from Drake," Allie said. "Well, I guess that wraps everything up. You're all up to date."

"Just one more question. Where should we go next?" Ingrid asked.

Allie shrugged. "I don't know. How about Rome or Paris like you wanted? We couldn't possibly get into trouble over there."

Ingrid smiled. "Well, we could try."

ABOUT THE AUTHOR

Dan DeKoning was born and raised in Milwaukee, Wisconsin, and currently lives in Knoxville, Tennessee with his wife and their cats.

He is a storyteller and poet who loves to write in a variety of genres and themes. He is also a voracious reader who loves to read anything he can get his hands on.

When he's not writing, you can find him hunting for treasures in used bookstores, or out exploring the planet, or geocaching, or searching for adventures and stories to tell.

ALSO BY DAN DEKONING

This is Dan DeKoning's complete library at the time of publication, but Dan has new books coming out all the time. Sign up for his newsletter at DanDeKoning.com to stay up to date on new releases.

<u>Fiction</u>
Déjà Vu
The Haunting of Hyacinth House
How Deep the Darkness

<u>Geocaching Mystery Series</u>
The Cacheland Conspiracy
The Quincy Bay Quandary
The Secret of the Seven Valleys
The Geocaching Mystery Omnibus – Volume 1

<u>Codi Cassidy Cozy Mystery Series</u>
Acoustics and Alibis
Ballads and Bloodshed
Codas and Calibers
Codi Cassidy Omnibus – Volume 1

<u>Poetry Collections</u>
Lost and Found
Random Thoughts